"You feel attuned to Pillatoro, don't you?"

In the darkness Jessica could just see Gideon's mouth curve as he spoke.

His fingers brushed the long silky tresses that fell across her shoulder. "I-It's a fantastic place. Like another world," she stammered, although she knew he meant more than that.

"And Luisa's room? Do you feel at home there?"

She ___ m more abo ___ oro had been ___ w I shou ___ lace for a—"

"For a woman who loves it? That's the only important thing, Jessica. Luisa's room has been empty too long. You'll breathe life into it, just as you..."

He lightly caressed the curve of her cheek before tilting her chin. Jessica couldn't speak. She no longer wanted to know why he'd given her the room. She didn't care as long as she could stay here....

EMMA DARCY nearly became an actress until her fiancé declared he preferred to attend the theater *with* her. She became a wife and mother. Later she took up oil painting—unsuccessfully, she remarks. Then she tried architecture, designing the family home in New South Wales. Next came romance writing—"the hardest and most challenging of all the activities," she confesses.

Books by Emma Darcy

HARLEQUIN PRESENTS

903—MAN IN THE PARK
921—A WORLD APART
935—THE IMPOSSIBLE WOMAN
960—WOMAN OF HONOUR
984—DON'T ASK ME NOW
999—THE UNPREDICTABLE MAN
1020—THE WRONG MIRROR
1033—THE ONE THAT GOT AWAY
1048—STRIKE AT THE HEART
1080—THE POSITIVE APPROACH

HARLEQUIN ROMANCE

2900—BLIND DATE

Don't miss any of our special offers. Write to us at the following address for information on our newest releases.

Harlequin Reader Service
901 Fuhrmann Blvd., P.O. Box 1397, Buffalo, NY 14240
Canadian address: P.O. Box 603,
Fort Erie, Ont. L2A 5X3

EMMA DARCY

mistress of pillatoro

Harlequin Books

TORONTO • NEW YORK • LONDON
AMSTERDAM • PARIS • SYDNEY • HAMBURG
STOCKHOLM • ATHENS • TOKYO • MILAN

Harlequin Presents first edition September 1988
ISBN 0-373-11103-7

Original hardcover edition published in 1987
by Mills & Boon Limited

Printed in U.S.A.

CHAPTER ONE

IT was finished.

No mistake.

No reprieve.

The telephone on Rex's desk buzzed and he snatched it up. Jessica watched him with bleak, empty eyes. It could only be Dawn on the other end of the line—Dawn of the silky voice and sexy body—the all-purpose secretary. No doubt she knew what had been going on in this office. Humiliation added another edge to Jessica's pain. She did not hear what was said. Rex put the telephone down and his eyes stabbed impatience at her.

'Cavilha has arrived. I can't keep him waiting. Yes or no, Jessica?'

There was no point in fighting it. Rex had made that eminently clear. One way or another he would force her out of the history department. Out of the university altogether. Professor Rex Anderson had the power and the influence to manipulate anything he wanted. She had to go somewhere else.

'Yes,' she whispered faintly.

'Sensible,' he muttered, then swept her with a critical gaze. 'A pity you can't do something about your hair. It hardly projects a professional image.'

A cracked little laugh that was more of a whimper slid out of her throat. She had left the thick, long fall of ash-blonde hair loose because there had been a time when Rex had loved it that way. Now it was only an irritation.

He shot her a baleful look as he pressed a buzzer attached to the telephone. 'Just watch yourself with Cavilha, Jessica. He's not a man I care to offend.'

She pushed herself out of the chair and moved aside with as much dignity as she could muster. Some defence mechanism inside her erected a very solid wall between herself and the rest of the world before Dawn showed in Rex's visitor. Dawn's look of gloating triumph didn't even touch her. She saw the man who entered as from a great distance.

He was tall and dark, the tailored perfection of his pin-striped suit emphasising the innate elegance of the man. There was an aloofness about his person, an aura of reserve that proclaimed him untouchable, inviolable, remote from everything and everybody else. A born aristocrat.

Jessica watched his gaze sweep the room, dismissing it with careless arrogance. The dark eyes suddenly locked on to hers. Immured in a numbness that should have been proof against anything, Jessica was completely unprepared for the force that hit her. Those eyes held a devouring knowledge that no human being should ever have. They reached into her, penetrating her defences with nerve-shattering directness, reading what should have remained hidden.

Jessica's heart squeezed into a tight, painful little ball. She wanted to look away. She didn't want him to see the emptiness in her soul, the bleak desolation that now ruled her life, and she knew that he did see it. No one should have that power. Her mind frantically reasoned that she was imagining it, yet she could not drag her gaze from his.

It was he who released her. The blazing intensity of his eyes was abruptly switched off, withdrawn behind impenetrable shutters of darkness. He looked away and it seemed that she no longer existed. It gave her a strange, hollow feeling and Jessica tried to shake it off.

Rex was greeting the man, holding out his hand, oozing his usual charm. 'May I offer you a drink— Scotch, brandy perhaps?'

'No, thank you.' A look of cold distaste flickered on the austere countenance as he quickly detached his hand from Rex's grasp, almost with an air of antipathy. 'I have very little time. I'd be obliged if you'd tell me whether or not you've found the person I want. Or do I have to go overseas to obtain someone suitable?'

'No, not at all. Miss Trelawney will take your project on. I was just finalising the matter with her before you arrived.'

Rex turned to her and she could see he was inwardly bristling at the other man's peremptory manner. Rex was used to people wanting to bask in his charm and he didn't like the sense of being dismissed as of no account. He performed the introduction with an uncharacteristic brusqueness. 'Jessica, this is Mr Cavilha...Miss Jessica Trelawney.'

A line cut down between the man's straight black eyebrows. 'What are her qualifications?'

The question was rapped out to Rex as if Jessica didn't exist. The hollow feeling grew worse.

'Absolutely first class,' Rex responded, injecting a note of enthusiasm into the words, obviously eager to palm her off on to someone else. Anyone else, so long as she wasn't under his and Dawn's noses. 'Jessica has a master's degree in history and has been assisting me in research. You couldn't get anyone better. I have personally tutored her in everything she knows.'

Pain shot through her numbness. He had tutored her all right, tutored her all the way up to this point of devastating rejection, and the glibness of his speech was somehow more wounding than anything that had gone before.

'I'll make my own assessment, thank you. Could you leave us alone now, or organise somewhere private...?'

'You're welcome to use my office.' Rex switched on a gracious smile. 'I have some work to do with my secretary. I'm sure you'll find everything satisfactory, and if you have the time afterwards, I'd like to discuss my application for a grant from the Cavilha Foundation.'

If anything, the smile drew only a more haughty reserve from the man. 'I'm very pressed for time today. We'll talk about it on some more appropriate occasion.'

'At your convenience, Mr Cavilha.'

Jessica had never heard of the Cavilha Foundation, but it had to be something big for Rex to be so obsequious to the man. No persuasion was attempted. Rex left without another word, abandoning Jessica without even a backward glance. For all he cared she could be left behind with a pack of wolves, and this Cavilha man exuded the type of power that could tear a person to pieces.

Jessica dragged her gaze back from the closed door, bleakly acknowledging the fact that Rex's door would always be closed to her from now on. The man was observing her sharply again. Those dark, penetrating eyes were midnight-blue; unfathomable pools which revealed nothing of what he was thinking. He moved with a lithe grace, propping himself against the desk and folding his arms. His face was still unsmiling, completely reserved.

'Please sit down, Miss Trelawney,' he commanded more than invited.

She moved stiffly back to the chair she had vacated for him. She sat down and returned his gaze steadily, much like a condemned prisoner awaiting sentence from the judge.

'Apparently you have Professor Anderson's trust and confidence, Miss Trelawney, but are you any good?' he asked quietly.

She forced herself to answer. 'I consider myself competent at carrying out historical research.' Probably not at anything else, she added defeatedly to herself.

'I don't want mere competence, Miss Trelawney. I want someone with the kind of inspiration that can find what has never been found before.'

A blanket of weariness settled on her mind. He wanted the impossible. 'I doubt that anyone can promise inspiration, Mr Cavilha. Or order it. I don't know what you're looking for, but it may not be there to be found, and if that is so, no amount of inspiration will find it.'

He gave no hint of reaction to her answer. His expression remained completely inscrutable. 'Tell me what you know about the early Spanish and Portuguese Pacific explorers.'

Jessica tried to gather her wits together. The question was so general and not directed at her own area of expertise. 'There was Pedro de Queiros...'

'In depth?'

It was no use. She just couldn't pull out the information he wanted. 'Virtually nothing,' she confessed flatly.

'Then you're not what I want.' He straightened up, so cool, so detached, so absolutely impersonal. 'There is no point in prolonging this interview. Good day, Miss Trelawney.'

He was going, and Jessica's future loomed in front of her as a huge bottomless hole with her spiralling down it for ever. She climbed unsteadily to her feet and turned towards the man who was already reaching for the doorknob. He was her only chance, the one person who could offer her an immediate escape from the consequences of loving Rex Anderson.

'Mr Cavilha...' Tears welled up in her eyes as he looked back at her, his expression one of impatience at being delayed. Despair forced her to speak. 'I...I can do a quick study. And I...I need the job. I know that's no recommendation, but I am skilled at research and...'

He didn't want her. The awful hopelessness of the situation overtook her. The tears spilled down her cheeks and she bit her lips to keep a sob from escaping. She bent her head, submitting to the inevitable.

She did not see him step back towards her, was not even aware of him until his hand gently squeezed her shoulder. 'Surely the position can't mean that much to you.'

She lifted her head and his stern face wobbled through a veil of uncontrollable tears, somehow demanding a response from her. Words spilled from her lips, words she hadn't meant to say but which were uppermost in her mind. 'I've . . . I've just lost someone I loved and I can't . . . I can't . . .' She turned away, covering her face with her hands as sobs racked her body. It didn't matter what he thought. Nothing mattered any more.

'I know how that feels.' It was barely a murmur, and Jessica felt the tone of sympathy rather than heard the words.

It only deepened her sense of loss. She cried even more helplessly, her whole body going into spasms of upheaval. She could not have resisted the tug of the strong arms which wound around her, even if she had wanted to. She sagged against a rocklike chest as he turned her around, and a firm, comforting hand pressed her head on to his shoulder. He caressed the long, flowing richness of her hair with soft, calming strokes which gradually gentled her sobs. Even when there were no more tears left she lay limply against him, too drained to move from an embrace which seemed so like a haven of peace.

She saw the door open, but her eyes were too glazed really to comprehend what it meant. Rex appeared, his face set in genial concern. 'I wanted to know if . . .' He stopped in mid-sentence, shock overriding concern as he took in the scene.

'Please go.' The words were quietly spoken but, despite the fact that the man who was holding her did not move, did not even turn his head towards the intrusion, his voice projected absolute authority.

Jessica saw chagrin bite into Rex's face. He glared at her, his expression changing to one of monumental affront. 'God damn it, Jessica! Have you no sense of...'

'Get out!'

The command sliced across the room like a deadly whiplash. Jessica saw it slap Rex's face into a deeper affront.

'You little slut!' The words were bitten out even as he retreated, slamming the door shut with uncommon haste.

The nasty slur on her character jolted Jessica out of her passivity. She lifted her head back, embarrassment burning colour into her pale cheeks as she forced herself to meet the gaze of the man who still held her. An apology quivered on her tongue but did not find voice. His eyes drained her of all initiative. Nothing needed to be said. He knew what she was feeling, and for one heart-thumping moment, Jessica knew an empathy that swirled beyond the barriers of reason.

'All right now?' he asked softly.

She nodded. Somehow this man had given her the strength to stand alone.

He withdrew, both mentally and physically, walking over to the window where he stared down at the quadrangle below for long, silent minutes. Jessica simply stared after him, feeling too dazed and confused to think. She heard the carillon playing in the tower and wondered why it should be ringing at this time of day. It slowly echoed into silence.

The man's stillness was finally broken by a little shake of his head. He turned around, his remoteness re-established. His eyes ran quickly over her, making a physical appraisal as if seeing her for the first time...a tall, slim girl, well proportioned in a feminine sense; a long, graceful neck; a pale oval face with the kind of features one sees in a Botticelli painting: finely arched brows, heavy-lidded wide blue eyes, a slightly long nose, and a small, beautifully shaped mouth. His gaze lingered a moment on the heavy fall of ash-blonde hair which reached almost to her waist.

Jessica tried to take a more objective view of him but found him a difficult man to assess. Not handsome in the genial way that Rex was handsome. The planes of his face were harsh, set in their own unique mould of strength and controlled power.

'What are you doing for the next three weeks?' he asked curtly.

'I...I don't know,' Jessica stammered, finding her voice with some difficulty. Her mind slowly moved into gear, throwing out the cruel necessities that Rex had forced on her. 'I have to find somewhere to live. I can't stay...where I've been any more.'

He took a pen from his pocket, took up a sheet of notepaper from Rex's desk and wrote on it. He handed it to her. 'Go there. I have a permanent reservation kept for me so you might as well use it. I'll be in New Zealand for the next few weeks and Samson won't be back from his tour until then.' A faint smile curved his lips. 'You can use the time to study. When I return I'll pick you up and see what you've been able to learn.'

'Pick me up? Where will we be going?' Jessica asked, somewhat dazed by the quick string of decisions.

'To Pillatoro, of course.' He strode to the door, throwing her a look which held a gleam of self-mockery. 'I'll give you the chance to prove yourself. For the present, at least, you've got the job.'

He was gone before she could utter a word to thank him. Through the opened door she saw Rex start away from Dawn's desk. 'Mr Cavilha...'

'Send your submission to the chairman of the Foundation. It'll get a fair hearing,' the hard voice said evenly. 'I have to be gone. I've a plane to catch at four-fifteen and I'm already running late. Thank you for your time and trouble.'

Rex stood stunned into immobility for several seconds. Dawn said something and he waved a dismissive hand at her. Then he turned and strode into his office, directing a glowering frown at Jessica as he shut the door. 'Did he give you the job?'

'Yes,' she answered, still not quite believing it herself. Too much had happened too quickly, and at the moment, nothing seemed very real, not even Rex.

His gaze flickered with annoyance as it ran over her, taking in the mussed strands of hair hanging over her shoulders. He heaved a sigh that sounded like frustration and constructed a smile of appeasement as he approached her. His hands gestured an appeal for patience and understanding.

'Jessica ... I think I might be making the most God almighty mistake. Let's just take a little while to think about what we're doing.' His hands closed around her upper arms, persuasively kneading the soft flesh.

Jessica's blood ran cold as she saw the shifting calculation in his eyes. Suddenly her mind was very, very clear. Rex had misread the embrace he had seen. He thought Mr Cavilha had taken a fancy to her and actually wanted her as a woman. And because Mr Cavilha had apparently found her desirable, Rex was wondering if he was letting go something of value, something he should keep around for himself.

Jessica shrank out of his grasp. 'You chose Dawn, Rex,' she bit out icily. 'I'll see that all my possessions are out of your house before tonight.'

'Now hold on a minute, Jessica. I know you haven't anywhere else to go.' His voice was all charm again for her. 'I'm sure we can work something out.'

To suit him! It hadn't worried him before that she didn't have a place to go. He wasn't thinking of her. He was only thinking of himself. The pride she had crushed for the sake of love stirred inside her and gathered strength, sending a scathing reply off her tongue.

'I'm not interested in a *ménage à trois*, Rex. I never would be. I hope you'll find whatever it is you want with Dawn. I promise you, you won't see me again.'

And pride stiffened her backbone enough for her to sweep out of the room, head held high. She was extremely thankful that Rex did not follow her to her office because the tears started again as she cleaned out her desk. All that she had lived for, hoped for, planned for...was finished. Rex had crushed her love and her promising career at the university. He had cut her adrift and now she didn't belong anywhere.

There was nothing for her to go back to in the mining city of Broken Hill where she had been born and brought up. She had left it when she finished school, rebelling against her parents' old-fashioned prejudice that further education was wasted on a girl. The one time she had returned home she had felt an alien within the family circle, a focal point for disapproval and criticism. The last five and a half years had been spent at Sydney University, thanks to Rex's influence. She was an academic, not suited for anything else but historical research.

If Mr Cavilha had not changed his mind...a little shiver ran down her spine. Why had it happened? She remembered the strong comfort imparted by his embrace. She was sure he was not a man who could easily be moved from his purpose by a woman's tears, yet he had given her his trust and a lifeline to some future.

Jessica unfolded the sheet of paper he had handed her, suddenly anxious to know where she would be going. As she read the note a sense of unreality gripped her again. With formal precision he had written, 'Miss Jessica Trelawney is to have the exclusive use of my executive suite at the Regent Hotel until the twenty-first of October, at my expense— Gideon Cavilha.'

The Regent! It was the best hotel in Sydney, its rooms reputed to be around two hundred dollars a night. She had no idea what an executive suite was worth. Her dazed eyes fastened on the signature. Gideon Cavilha. Gideon…somehow it suited him. But who was he? What was he?

A name drifted into her mind…Pillatoro. That was where he was going to take her, but she had never heard of the place. Jessica slowly folded the note and carefully tucked it away in her handbag. Wherever it was, whatever it meant, she would go to Pillatoro. With Gideon Cavilha.

By the time Jessica arrived at the Regent Hotel, she was worn out both physically and emotionally. All she wanted to do was collapse on a bed. The taxi-driver carried in her two suitcases and a porter was summoned to collect the five cartons of books and notes. They were all she owned apart from her clothes. The shabby heap of luggage looked hopelessly incongruous in such a place as this but Jessica was past caring about what other people thought.

Nevertheless, as weary as she was, a prickle of apprehension ran down her spine as she presented Gideon Cavilha's note at the reception desk. To her relief there were no questions or eyebrows raised. The name of Gideon Cavilha summoned immediate VIP treatment. Two porters collected her luggage, she was personally escorted to the executive suite, offered every type of service that could be thought of, asked what time she would like breakfast brought to her, and assured that her every need would be catered for. She had only to ask.

Jessica was dazed enough by the service, but the spacious luxury of Gideon Cavilha's suite represented another world to her. The step between the middle-class appointments of Rex's home and this hotel was gigantic. She took off her shoes and padded around barefoot on the thick, peach-coloured carpet. The cream and tan tonings of all the furnishings provided the kind of setting that Jessica had only ever imagined in Hollywood.

But once the lights were out and Jessica was very alone in the king-size bed, all the luxury in the world could not appease her inner misery. A clean break, Rex had called it, but the reality was more like brutal surgery, and disillusionment did not take away the pain of his betrayal and rejection.

She had been so sure that Rex loved her, never doubting that their relationship would lead to the marriage he had promised. She had believed his insistence that it was for her sake alone that they live together for a year before tying the legal knot. Rex was eighteen years older than herself and he had wanted her to be certain of her commitment to him. But he had never meant to marry her. Jessica realised it now, and the tears that dampened her pillow held the sting of bitterness.

For the last two days she had been holding on to the feeble hope that he didn't mean what he had said. She had told herself that Dawn had seduced him. It was only a matter of waiting out a stupid mistake. But she had been fooling herself, fooling herself all along. Rex could not have had any real feeling for her or he would not have done what he did—dismiss her as though she were a servant who was no longer convenient, threatening her career if she refused to take the job with Cavilha.

Gideon Cavilha...

Pillatoro...

Tantalising names...heralding the future, whatever that might be. She could not bring herself to care. Yet as she finally drifted into sleep it was not Rex's cruel betrayal that lingered in Jessica's mind, but the pillarlike strength of her new employer.

CHAPTER TWO

THE three weeks were up. Jessica had received no word from Gideon Cavilha, but it was the twenty-first of October and she did not doubt that he would arrive at the Regent Hotel some time today. For some reason she trusted his word implicitly.

Jessica took great pains over her appearance, intent on correcting the poor first impression she had surely made. Her pale grey suit was smartly professional, teamed with a tailored pink blouse and plain black high-heels. Her long hair was smoothly confined to a high coil around her crown, her only make-up a soft pink lipstick.

She was considerably more composed, more self-assured, and more ready to confront Gideon Cavilha than she had been on that traumatic afternoon in Rex's office. Then she had been suffering from shock, which undoubtedly accounted for the deranged fancy that in one glance he had seen all there was to know about her. He might be a rich, powerful man with unusual force of character, but she did not believe he had any such extraordinary powers.

She waited. At lunch time she ordered sandwiches and coffee to be brought to her room. The afternoon hours passed with agonising slowness. Jessica could not settle to reading and did not wish to be found watching television. She sat at the window, taking in the view of Sydney Harbour but paying little attention to it. The sun set. Twilight spread fingers of darkness around the harbour while another kind of darkness crept into Jessica's soul. What if Gideon Cavilha didn't come...

She knew so little about the man. She had discovered that the Cavilha Foundation provided grants for academic research, but if there was any printed information on Gideon Cavilha himself, it had eluded her.

She had not liked to ask any questions about him of the hotel staff, although clearly he was well known to them, and highly respected since she had been treated with the utmost deference and courtesy. She remembered his aristocratic manner, that air of having been born to generations of wealth, the sheer presence of the man that had made her feel... not alone.

And she wasn't alone now. She hadn't heard him come in, but Jessica suddenly knew that Gideon Cavilha was in the room with her. She turned her head quickly, her gaze drawn unerringly to where he stood near the door. His stillness caught at her heart, squeezing it tightly. Then, in an abrupt, decisive movement, his hand lifted to snap on the overhead light.

He was exactly as she remembered him: aloof, reserved, unsmiling, yet the power radiating from him diminished everyone and everything else; a man who was master of his own destiny, and that of others.

'Are you ready to go?' The words were softly spoken, more a statement than an enquiry.

'Yes,' she replied.

She didn't even question the lack of greeting from either of them. Somehow it seemed unnecessary.

He was here and she was ready to go with him. It was as simple as that. He walked towards her. She stood up.

'Have they looked after you properly here?' he asked. The very tone of his voice suggested that if she had any criticism at all of the hotel staff, action would be taken.

Her hands lifted in an instinctive gesture of helplessness. 'It was so generous of you. I don't know what I would have done... I don't know how to thank you.'

He stepped closer, taking her hands in his. He looked tired and drawn, which surprised Jessica. Without having given it much thought, she had visualised him as being indestructible. The dark eyes seemed softer, kinder than she remembered them.

'And your grief?' he asked gently.

The period of time during which Rex had been the focus of her life seemed to recede into the distant past. The hurt of his rejection was still a scar on her heart but her dependence on his love had entirely evaporated. 'It's well under control,' she answered, half incredulous that it was so, but knowing that she spoke the truth. Somehow this man had supplied her with the strength to do it.

His mouth curved ever so slightly, as if her answer pleased him, but his hands released hers and dropped to his side and she sensed his formidable reserve slipping back into place. 'Did you manage to learn anything useful these last three weeks?' His voice was suddenly flat, without emotion.

'All I could find on the subject at the Mitchell Library,' Jessica assured him. 'You didn't tell me the specifics of the research I'm to do for you,' she added questioningly.

He turned away, moving across the room towards the telephone table. The action was so deliberate that Jessica felt he was consciously putting distance between them as he replied. 'My father formulated a theory about the discovery of the east coast of Australia that goes against traditional views. He died before he completed his studies. It will be your duty to finish his work.'

A prickle of unease ran down Jessica's back. Duty, not job. That was not how historical research was done. It had to be carried out without any bias towards any one point of view. 'What was your father's theory?' she asked, too troubled to let the matter drop.

'He believed that the first explorer of the East Coast of Australia was a Portuguese navigator, Pedro de Sequeira, who discovered it centuries earlier than Cook.'

Jessica had come across that general theory during her study at the Mitchell Library. There was a considerable amount of circumstantial evidence to support a Portuguese discovery, but nothing she had read had named Pedro de Sequeira as the man most likely to have been the navigator in question.

'You will have all my father's notes to work from,' Gideon Cavilha continued. He turned, his eyes stabbing back at her as he picked up the telephone. 'You can employ the same archivists he directed in France, Spain, Portugal, England, and of course here, in Australia. I will supply interpreters when you need them. Cost is no object. The proof has to be found.' He paused, his gaze boring into

her, drilling a test of her mettle as he added, 'Are
you capable of organising and conducting such a
search?'

Jessica didn't hesitate. 'Yes, but I can't promise
that you'll get the answer you want,' she added
cautiously.

His whole bearing stiffened into haughty arrogance. 'My father's belief is correct. Your job is to
prove it. Nothing else.'

A shaft of fear sliced through her, but everything
she had been taught rebelled against his edict. 'That
is not the purpose of research, Mr Cavilha,' she
said quietly.

'It is my purpose, Miss Trelawney,' he stated
flatly. 'You have three months to prove your worth.
After that time you will be asked to remain or go,
depending on your showing.'

So she was on trial, Jessica thought with a sinking
heart. Very much on trial since she had had the
temerity to raise professional integrity. Gideon
Cavilha apparently took her silence to mean ac-
quiescence to his will, for he proceeded to put in a
service call for porters.

Jessica turned her head away and stared miserably out of the window. She wondered if Rex had
known the precise details of the job, if he had deliberately set her up in a project that could not lead
to success. Not that it mattered now. There was no
other choice but to give it her best shot.

She stole a covert glance at her new employer.
He seemed sunk in thought, contemplating some
private problem. His austere countenance did not
invite conversation. No doubt he had given her the
job against his better judgement and was probably

regretting the compassionate impulse. There was certainly no sense of intimate understanding between them now, and Jessica wondered if her own fraught state of nerves had conjured it up. Common sense assured her that any personal friendship with this man was impossible anyway. He was far removed from her station in life and it was better that he remain so.

The porters arrived. Jessica motioned them to her suitcases and boxes in the bedroom. Gideon Cavilha frowned after them as they trolleyed out the luggage. He glanced sharply at her. 'That is all you have?' He sounded appalled at the paucity of her possessions.

If Jessica had needed any reminder of the difference between their stations in life, his comment certainly underlined it. Her chin lifted in aggressive pride, refusing any apology for the limitations of her life. 'Yes. That's all I have,' she asserted with an innate sense of personal dignity.

'Forgive me,' he said quietly. 'Shall we go?'

His swift understanding embarrassed her. Again it seemed that he had looked into her soul and read all that was there, and Jessica felt extremely agitated that he should find her so transparent. Should she go with him? But what other choice did she have? And she owed him for these last three weeks. Owed him for extricating her from the situation Rex had so meanly manoeuvred. The least she could do was work out the three months' trial.

With an air of decisive purpose, Jessica picked up the handbag she had left on the table and accompanied Gideon Cavilha out of the suite. He did not take her arm, did not touch her with even the slightest brush of hand or body as he escorted her to the elevator, yet his personal magnetism was so strong she felt drawn along within a powerful force-field.

They rode down in silence and walked straight through the reception area. A limousine stood waiting outside the hotel entrance and a uniformed chauffeur saw them both settled into the plush leather softness of the back seat. It was not until they were purring over the Sydney Harbour Bridge that Jessica found composure enough to speak naturally.

'You didn't tell me where Pillatoro is, Mr Cavilha.'

The austere lines of his face seemed to deepen. 'At the centre of my world,' he murmured, then as if acknowledging the obscurity of his reply he added, 'You will see soon enough. It's only a couple of hours away.'

Jessica did not feel encouraged to enquire further. The limousine rolled on through the northern suburbs, keeping to the Pacific Highway. Two hours would take them to the Central Coast if their route didn't deviate. At least it wasn't far from Sydney if she wanted to escape, Jessica thought, then be-rated herself for even thinking the word 'escape'. She was not a coward. If she wanted to leave Gideon Cavilha and Pillatoro she would do so openly and with proper notice.

The silence in the car had lasted so long that she was startled when Gideon Cavilha spoke again. 'I had an unusual request from the Cultural and Her-itage Commission today. That was one of the reasons I was delayed. Do you know anything about them?'

Rex! Jessica darted an apprehensive look at the man beside her. He was staring ahead, apparently unconcerned by the matter. It was surely an idle question, a simple connection of thought between heritage and her knowledge of history, yet she felt constrained to give him the one pertinent fact that was uppermost in her mind.

'Professor Rex Anderson is the chairman of the Cultural and Heritage Commission. He rules its policy. I know that,' she stated as evenly as she could.

'Aah,' he said, and lapsed into silence again.

Jessica shrank inside herself, worrying over this new development. Perhaps she was being over-sensitive where Rex was concerned but, whatever the request was from the Cultural and Heritage Commission, its timing was suspect. Maybe Rex intended to curry favour with Gideon Cavilha since he wanted a grant from the Cavilha Foundation. On the other hand, he hadn't liked Gideon Cavilha's manner to him and Jessica was all too well aware now that Rex had a mean, vindictive streak.

However, whatever Rex was up to, Jessica decided there was nothing she could do about it. Her involvement with him was over. She hoped Gideon Cavilha had not connected her to Rex in any but a professional sense. She would hate him to know how stupid she had been. She vowed she would never be caught in such a self-defeating relationship again.

Her inner tension slowly eased. Jessica was glad of Gideon Cavilha's silence. After a while she could even ignore his presence. She watched the passing landscape as if it was a series of backdrops representing the shift from past to future: the impressive fiords of the Hawkesbury River, the lush bushland around Moonee, the glittering expanse of Brisbane Water around which Gosford City nestled. They skirted Gosford and soon left the outlying suburbs behind, heading for the coast.

Jessica had stopped wondering where Pillatoro was, but curiosity stirred again as she noticed they had left all signs of habitation behind. A full moon cast an eerie light over the wild bushland. The headlights of the limousine picked out a sign announcing Bouddi National Park, then shortly afterwards the car slowed and took a steep, narrow, winding road down through the natural bushland.

'This is where we live,' Gideon Cavilha suddenly announced.

'In a national park?' Jessica observed in surprise.

He smiled. It was the first time Jessica had ever seen him smile and in an instant the sense of separation was wiped out.

'My great-great-grandfather, Rafael Cavilha, built Pillatoro well over a hundred years ago, before the area was gazetted. It now has the advantage of being one of the few places in the world that can never be built out,' Gideon informed her.

It was information that relieved her mind. Australia was such a young country that any place of that age was classified as historic, and of natural interest to the Cultural and Heritage Commission.

Suddenly the bush was behind them and in front of them lay the moonlit waves of the Pacific Ocean. The road curved around a small bay where a large, white yacht rode at anchor, making the scene even more picturesque.

Gideon Cavilha leaned forward and tapped the glass partition behind the driver. Without a word having passed between them, the chauffeur pulled the limousine over to the verge of the road and parked. The dark gaze stabbed an invitation—or was it a challenge?—at Jessica, as Gideon Cavilha opened his own door. 'You can see from here,' he said, and stepped out of the car without waiting for her reply.

The door was left open for her to follow, and Jessica followed automatically, pulled by a strong sense of anticipation that she didn't stop to question. Gideon Cavilha closed the door after her, shutting off the car's interior light. He curved one arm around her shoulders, turning her to face the east, and his other arm pointed upwards. 'There, at the top of the headland,' he murmured.

Jessica was extremely conscious of his closeness and wished he would move away. She tried to ignore the disturbing power of his presence and swung her gaze upwards, following the sheer line of cliff which rose from a curiously flat platform of rocks. She had nursed no particular expectation of the Cavilha home, but what she saw caught the breath in her throat.

It was not a house or a mansion or a castle. She could not find a name for it. It grew out of the top of the cliff and it was impossible to discern where natural rock ended and the great sandstone and concrete structure began. It rose in colonnaded terraces, vaguely Mediterranean in style, yet too massive to be called a villa. It looked formidable, yet beautiful in a strange, primeval sense...like a thrusting, belligerent monument of man's power to sit astride his world.

As Jessica stared at it she was conscious of an odd stirring in her heart, a tug that she could not explain on any level of common sense. All she knew was that there was something about that extraordinary structure which struck some deep, inner chord in her, awakening an anticipation of...of something she could not define...something that tied in with the strange effect that Gideon Cavilha had on her.

And without turning her head she knew he was watching her. She could feel that dark, compelling gaze on her, waiting to see...waiting for her to show him what she felt. Some sixth sense told her that this was indeed the centre of his world...the heart of whatever it was that drove him to be the man he was.

'It must mean something...the name, Pillatoro,' she observed, wanting, needing to know more about it.

'Yes. It comes from the Awabakal, the Aboriginal tribe that inhabited the area before the white man came. Pillatoro means to set; as in the sun and the moon and the stars.' He said the words with a soft resonance that suggested they held a poignant meaning for him.

'It's beautiful,' Jessica whispered.

'Yes.'

The hand on her shoulder shifted. It curved around her head, turning it, forcing her to meet his gaze. There was almost a barbaric arrogance in the action, yet Jessica couldn't find the will to fight it.

'Jessica...'

The hand left her head and gently brushed her cheek. The gesture was strangely like a salute; tender, respectful, a mark of acceptance that also carried a touch of ownership. 'Welcome to Pillatoro, Jessica.'

Her heart hammered around her chest. It was incredibly difficult to fight off the sheer magnetism of the man. It frightened her that she actually wanted to be passive, to submit to whatever his will dictated. And what kind of mess would that land her into? Hadn't her experience with Rex taught her anything?

Gideon Cavilha shouldn't be touching her like this. It was directly personal and infinitely disturbing. She couldn't afford to let him touch her like this. He was her employer and she didn't want any kind of intimacy with him.

'Let's go home,' he murmured. His hand dropped to her elbow and he steered her back into the car. Jessica moved like a sleep-walker, too emotionally confused to resist. She pressed over to the far side of the seat and stared out of the window, trying to reassert her independence as the limousine purred into movement again.

A stone wall separated the Cavilha property from the bushland. The road wound upwards, past clumps of exotic trees, orchards, gardens which spilled over clusters of rocks. Everywhere Jessica looked there was an air of wildness, barely tamed yet under firm control. It was unlike any parkland or garden Jessica had ever seen, yet it was right, so right that her heart pulsed with excitement as they neared the top.

They passed through the gateway of another, higher wall, flanked by lions cut from stone. It guarded the entrance to a huge, flagstoned courtyard. The chauffeur wheeled the limousine into a U-turn which brought them to a halt in front of a bank of steps that ran the width of the courtyard. Jessica's gaze followed the wide, gently ascending flight up to the colonnaded terrace where a great archway framed the entrance doors to the Cavilha home. It was built entirely of dressed sandstone, covered in places by rambling rose bushes which took blossoms almost to the roofline.

Gideon Cavilha opened her door. She looked up and had to fight the feeling of being trapped. It was terribly unnerving and her legs shook a little as she alighted and stood beside him.

'I'll take you in and introduce you to Mrs Price who looks after the running of the house. She'll see you settled into your room.'

The words were matter-of-fact. Ordinary. She took a grain of comfort from them. 'Thank you,' she murmured, knowing in her heart that there was nothing ordinary here; not this man nor this place.

He gestured for her to accompany him up the steps and once again she walked beside him without touching, yet inexorably bound to his path. He opened one of the huge entrance doors and stood back to let her pass through. It was like stepping into another world... another time... another life, and Jessica had the wild impression that she was walking into something inescapable, from which it was already too late to draw back.

CHAPTER THREE

THE entrance hallway was long and wide, of cathedral proportions. At its end was a wall of stained glass, depicting a scene which obviously had some religious significance, although Jessica could not place it. The sheer artistry of it was breathtaking enough, but the multi-hued pattern of light it threw on to the floor-tiles was pure magic. Jessica was so enraptured by it that Gideon Cavilha's voice sounded merely like background music.

'These doors on the left lead to my home offices and also to the library where you will be working. To the right is the music-room and Sam's offices. Pillatoro is a huge complex and it might take you a while to find your way around it.'

Below the stained-glass mural was a broad staircase which took them down to a lower level, on to a huge octagonal mezzanine floor which was dominated by a central fountain made in the same shape. Around it were massed ferns, orchids, and a great number of exotic plants that Jessica could not identify.

There were staircases leading off the floor to the right and left, but beyond the fountain were steps that led down to what looked like a ballroom which seemed to run right to the cliff-edge. Its immensely tall windows offered an amazing vista of ocean and horizon from all three sides. To step from the cathedral quality of the hall, and its stained glass window, to this ... Jessica simply shook her head, dazed beyond thought.

A plump, middle-aged woman bustled up the stairs from the right, straightening her skirt as if she had just torn off an apron. She beamed a welcome at Jessica as Gideon introduced her. 'You'll look after Miss Trelawney, won't you, Mrs Price?'

'Of course, Mr Gideon,' came the rather breathy response.

'Miss Trelawney is to have Luisa's room.'

Jessica saw the look of surprise—astonishment—flicker over the housekeeper's face. It took the woman a moment to recover herself. 'Just as you say, Mr Gideon. It's good to have you back home again.'

He nodded. 'Is Sam home?'

'Yes, he's in the music-room, I think.'

'I was!'

The soft, richly cultured voice seemed to echo through the hall, filling all its space and vibrating down the staircase to curl around them and turn them towards it.

'I thought I heard you come in, Gideon, and I couldn't wait to see you.'

Gideon laughed, his whole face softening into lines of pleasure. 'I think they're my words, Sam. It's great to have you back home.'

Jessica was so startled by the change in Gideon's demeanour that she could not help staring at him. It was like looking at another man altogether, one who was warm and benevolent and stunningly handsome.

'And who have we here?'

The voice drew Jessica's gaze away from Gideon and her eyes widened in surprise at the huge giant of a man who stood at the top of the stairs, looking down at them. His mane of red-gold hair and bristling beard were startling enough, but they only added the impact of barbaric colour to his massive size.

His shirt was unbuttoned to the waist, his white dungarees rolled up to the calves of his strongly muscled legs. He was not so very tall, perhaps only just topping six feet, but he carried himself tall: his imposing head thrust back, his massive shoulders squared, his huge barrel chest thrust out. He looked for all the world like a wild, rollicking buccaneer from another century altogether, and his eyes were twinkling down at Jessica as if she were prize booty.

'This is Miss Jessica Trelawney, who will be carrying on our father's research. My brother, Samson, Jessica.'

She heard the more formal note of restraint in Gideon's voice but Jessica could not tear her gaze away from Samson as he came down the stairs.

His eyes were caressing her, drinking in everything about her. 'If Gideon had told me how beautiful you were, I would have been out in the courtyard to greet you,' he murmured.

'Sam...' It was a softly chiding sigh from Gideon.

A wide grin broke through the beard. 'I was expecting a dour, scholarly type, not...'

'Miss Trelawney does have the necessary qualifications,' Gideon said drily.

The grin softened to a smile of warm admiration as Sam's gaze returned to Jessica. 'More. Much

more,' he murmured, and took her hands in his. 'I
am delighted to meet you, Miss Tre-
lawney... Jessica...' He rolled her name out in his
beautiful, deep voice. 'While you are our guest here,
it will be my pleasure to help you in any way I can.
I look forward to knowing you...much better.'

His speech, his manner, everything about him
had a grandeur that struck Jessica so strongly that
she was speechless. They were so unalike, these
brothers, and yet...she looked at Gideon, so dark
and austere and once more cloaked in his aristocratic reserve...they both belonged to this extraordinary place; Samson characterising the barbaric
splendour of Pillatoro in the same way as Gideon
characterised its power.

'Mrs Price, please take Miss Trelawney to her
room,' Gideon ordered abruptly, almost as if he
was impatient with the rather overwhelming attention his brother was giving to Jessica. 'It's been
a long day for her, and she must feel very tired,'
he added in a more moderate tone.

'Tomorrow you must tell me all about yourself,'
Sam said with sparkling anticipation as he released
her hands.

Jessica was finally able to find her tongue. 'It's
very kind of you,' she murmured, then looked
quickly at Gideon, hoping that he did not think she
was encouraging his brother. 'Thank you for
everything.'

His air was distinctly remote as he replied, 'I'll
see you in the morning, Miss Trelawney.' He took
a step back up the staircase and placed an authoritative hand on his brother's broad shoulder.
'Come, Sam, we have a great deal to catch up on.'

A touch on Jessica's arm dragged her gaze back to Mrs Price and, with an inviting smile, the housekeeper began to steer her towards the staircase on the left-hand side of the fountain. 'This passage leads to the bedroom wing,' she explained. 'On the other side of the house are the entertainment areas and the servants' quarters. I'm sure Mr Gideon will show you around in due course. For the moment I'll just take you to your room.'

Something nagged at the back of Jessica's mind, something driven into insignificance by the startling appearance of Samson Cavilha. It took her several moments to recall what it was...Luisa's room...and the housekeeper's astonished reaction to Gideon's statement that Jessica should have it.

She hesitated in her step, turning anxiously to the woman beside her. 'Mrs Price, I don't want to put anyone out. If Luisa would object to my having her room...'

The housekeeper shook her head. 'You won't be putting anyone out, dear. Luisa was Rafael Cavilha's wife, for whom Pillatoro was built. She died over a hundred years ago. The room has not been occupied since...' She paused, frowning as if conscious of some lapse in discretion. 'Anyhow, Mr Gideon said you were to have it,' she finished decisively.

Jessica wondered about the unfinished comment. The room that Rafael's wife had occupied...wouldn't that be a very special room? Jessica began to feel a distinct uneasiness. 'Is it wrong for me to be there, Mrs Price?' she asked bluntly.

The housekeeper sliced a sharp look at her. 'It's not for me to say, Miss Trelawney. I'm sure you're very welcome.'

Her mouth clamped into a thin line that told Jessica that no further comment would be forthcoming. Whatever Mrs Price thought of Gideon's orders, she was obviously not disposed to question them. She opened the door at the end of the passageway, and stood back for Jessica to enter first.

Jessica took one step inside and all the questions in her mind were blanked out. Her gaze swept around in dazed wonderment, feasting on the most richly furnished, the most exquisite, fascinating, beautiful room she had ever seen.

Everywhere there was magnificent craftsmanship, artistry of a bygone era. The richly polished wood of the chests of drawers and the secretaire held inlays of ivory and enamel. Magnificent tapestries hung on the walls. The double bed featured an imposing bedhead, elaborately carved with an intricate pattern of flowers and vines and trees, a design which was repeated in the massive marriage chest which stood at the foot of the bed, and in the door panels of the wardrobes.

The far wall of the room, which was obviously windowed for a view of the sea, was curtained in a heavy, ivory silk. The hand-crocheted lace of the bedspread was the same creamy shade. The carpet was mushroom-pink and the chairs had been upholstered in brocaded velvet; dark pink, gold and ivory. Jessica was so entranced that she barely noticed Mrs Price move past her.

'The en suite bathroom is just through here.' The housekeeper had opened another door and waved an invitation for Jessica to see for herself.

Jessica's stunned gaze swept over ivory tiles and slabs of marble which held a delicate flush of pink, mirrors framed in gold, ornate gold fittings everywhere... 'It's all so...so beautiful. Unbelievable,' she murmured, completely awe-struck.

'Yes,' the housekeeper nodded. 'Of course, the bathroom was modernised for the last Mrs Cavilha, and the carpet in the bedroom has been renewed from time to time, but...'

Mrs Cavilha...Luisa's room...the wife of Rafael Cavilha...the room for every Cavilha wife...Jessica's mind leapt through the connections and the reason for the housekeeper's reserve was suddenly very clear.

'Perhaps you would like to freshen up, Miss Trelawney. I'll go and see to your luggage, then bring you a supper-tray.'

Jessica put out a hand and halted her. She felt way out of depth in this extraordinary place and she needed to come to grips with what was going on around her. 'Please...be honest with me,' she appealed, almost in desperation. 'It doesn't seem right to you, does it? I'm just an employee, like you, and all this...it's too good for me. I shouldn't be here.'

The housekeeper looked searchingly at Jessica, then slowly shook her head as if she didn't know what to think. 'You're not like me, Miss Trelawney. The work Mr Gideon wants you to do is very important to him. It was all his father lived for, God rest his soul. Perhaps that's why...but

it's not for me to question Mr Gideon's reasons,'
she put in briskly. 'I can only tell you that up until
now, Luisa's room has always been reserved for the
mistress of Pillatoro.'

The mistress of Pillatoro...

Jessica rubbed at her forehead, trying to clear
her mind into a sane pattern of thought. What on
earth had she walked into? She couldn't take Luisa's
room, yet it was too late to protest against the ar-
rangement now. Tomorrow she would have to
broach the matter with Gideon, get it straightened
out. Clearly, if she stayed here, it could cause un-
pleasant speculation in the household.

Mrs Price gave her hand a kindly pat. 'Mr Gideon's right. You're tired. You just relax, dear, and
I'll bring you a nice pot of tea straight away.'

It wasn't fatigue, Jessica thought. Too much had
happened too fast. From the moment she had seen
Pillatoro she had felt overwhelmed by it and there
had been no respite since then, one climactic
impression crowding on another until she could
barely call her soul her own.

She felt curiously powerless to stop what was
happening to her, and hours later Jessica lay in bed,
wondering if it was possible to be seduced by a
room. She should have stopped Mrs Price from un-
packing her things and putting them away, but she
hadn't. She knew that she ought to insist to Gideon
Cavilha that she be moved somewhere else, yet to
move now would be a terrible wrench. Somehow
Luisa's room held the whole intriguing atmosphere
of Pillatoro, and Jessica loved it.

Sleep was hopelessly elusive. It wasn't only the
idea of Luisa's room that was disturbing; there was

the work that Gideon Cavilha wanted her to do. Mrs Price had said it was important to him; and he had called it 'her duty' to find the proof that had eluded his father. What if the task was impossible? She couldn't fake any proof that Gideon Cavilha wanted, no matter what the cost.

Jessica tried to calm herself, but finally an inner restlessness drove her out of bed. She padded across to the wall of curtains and opened them. A magnificent view of the ocean rushed in on her. She found the glass door which gave access to the balcony. Too large to be called a balcony, she thought, as she stepped outside and moved to the balustrade which stretched between the arches. The covered terrace ran the whole length of the bedroom wing.

She clung on to the railing and arched her back, letting the night breeze waft through her long hair. The restless movement of the sea suited her mood and she watched the dim moonlight flickering on the waves. Pillatoro means to set, as in the sun and the moon and the stars, she recalled with a deep satisfaction, and it did seem so very appropriate now. She lifted her gaze to the stars, brilliant dots in a dark, velvet sky.

She stood there for a long time, her spirits soothed in a way she would not have thought possible a short while ago. Footsteps echoed softly through her mind. She turned her head and saw Gideon Cavilha walking towards her. He passed in and out of the shadow of the arches, almost an unreal figure, yet emanating a powerful presence that held her transfixed, waiting for him in a stillness that permeated her soul.

'Can't you sleep?' The words were softly spoken, barely a breath of sound in the darkness. He loomed up beside her and a strange tingle of excitement ran through Jessica's body, making her feel slightly dizzy and breathless.

'I . . . I was restless.' It didn't even sound like her own voice. Why did this man have such a strong effect upon her?

It was too dark for her to see the expression in his eyes, but she saw his mouth curve as he spoke. 'Jessica . . .' The slow, sensual lilt he gave to her name raised goose-bumps on her skin. '. . . I saw you, soaking it in. You feel attuned to Pillatoro, don't you?'

His hand lifted, his fingers brushing the long silky tress of hair that fell across her shoulder. It seemed such a familiar, intimate gesture that Jessica's voice was momentarily paralysed. 'I . . . it's a fantastic place. Like another world,' she stammered out, although she knew he meant more than that.

'And Luisa's room? Do you feel at home there?'

The question that had pulsed in her mind spilled off her tongue. 'Why did you give it to me?'

The fingers were abruptly still. 'You don't like it?'

'I love it, but you know I shouldn't be there. It's not the place for a . . . for a . . .'

'For a woman who loves it? That's the only important thing, Jessica. Luisa's room has been empty too long. Empty of the life it should have. You'll breathe life into it, just as you . . .'

His hand lifted higher, lightly caressing the curve of her cheek before tilting her chin. Jessica could not speak. She knew he was going to kiss her. She felt choked by a wild mêlée of emotions as his head bent to hers. The touch of his lips sent a ripple of shock through her whole body, but she could not tear her mouth away.

It was not a kiss of love, nor of passion. It was more an experimental co-joining, of two streams of life meeting and tasting one another, questioning their compatibility to flow together. And the numbness that Rex had left in Jessica's soul was swept away by a wave of primitive vitality. Never had she felt so alive, so incredibly aware of herself as Gideon's mouth searched hers and she searched his, all inhibitions forgotten in this moment of discovery.

The tempestuous thundering of her heart was far more immediate than the noise of the waves beating against the base of the cliff. She wanted to touch Gideon, have him draw closer to her, enfold her against him as he had done on that first day in comfort, but it was not just comfort she wanted. Yet in another sense, she did not need his physical contact, because what passed between them was far more intimate.

His mouth withdrew from hers and they stood apart, staring at each other in the darkness. Jessica yearned to know what he had felt, but could not bring herself to ask, to break the throbbing silence. Was it her imagination or was his breathing a little deeper, a fraction faster? In the shadows of the night his face appeared unmoved, inscrutable. His lips moved slowly.

'There is "that power, which erring men call chance".'

Jessica's heart lurched in recognition of what he was saying. She knew those words. They had been written nearly three hundred years ago by the blind poet, Milton. And she had felt that power from her first meeting with Gideon Cavilha, a sense of lives linking in a predestined manner...linked even more forcefully when she lifted her eyes to Pillatoro and accepted a reality that was different from anything else.

She didn't understand it, and in a way it frightened her, but there seemed an inevitability about it that she couldn't fight. She shivered as she remembered that her only covering was a light silk nightie. If Gideon should choose to take advantage of her vulnerability, how was she going to resist his compelling attraction?

As if he sensed the apprehensive tumult in her mind, he moved back a pace, his hands dropping to his sides. He sucked in a deep breath and spoke in a whispering caress. 'Goodnight, Jessica. Sleep well now.' Then he turned on his heel and walked away, fading into the background of shadows.

His abrupt withdrawal was a relief, yet he left Jessica feeling totally limp, as if he had drained her of all purpose and taken it with him. It took a tremendous effort of will simply to return to her bed, and no sooner had Jessica hit the pillow than she fell into a deep, dreamless sleep.

CHAPTER FOUR

JESSICA did sleep well, but when she awoke to the bright light of morning, the memory of Gideon's kiss and her response to it was intensely disturbing. Here she was, living under his roof, ensconced in the room he had personally designated, an employee who had yet to prove her worth ... and what did such a man want of her? Why had he kissed her?

She had lost her head completely, that was certain. She had been out of her mind to let him assume any intimacy at all with her. The lateness of the hour, the strange mood engendered by the atmosphere of this extraordinary place, the odd restlessness of her soul ... none formed any good excuse for her crazy submissiveness. If Gideon Cavilha was entertaining any idea of enjoying a little dalliance with her while she was here, she would now have to correct him very firmly.

Jessica made up her mind that whatever happened here at Pillatoro, she was not going to become any man's mistress. Rex had fooled her with his talk of marriage, but common sense insisted that it would be even more foolish to form a relationship with either Gideon or Samson Cavilha. The wealth of Pillatoro was statement enough that a mere employee would be ineligible as far as marriage was concerned.

A knock on the door heralded a maid with an early morning pot of tea. She informed Jessica that breakfast would be brought to her in half an hour and Mr Gideon expected her in the library at nine o'clock. The avid assessment in her eyes told Jessica that she had become a prime target of curiosity in the household.

Determined on looking primly professional, Jessica dressed in a plain blue gabardine skirt and a long-sleeved tailored blouse whose only claim to femininity was the tiny print of pink and blue flowers. Her hair was very firmly pinned up into the usual, efficient coil on her crown. She even hesitated over applying lipstick, but feminine vanity finally insisted on it.

Determined to strip herself of all romantic illusions, Jessica deliberately chose the balcony-exit from her room. There was no moonlight now, no phantasms of the mind. The ocean glittered with sunlight, the sky was a clear blue, and while the architectural structure of Pillatoro was still mind-staggering, she told herself it was just sandstone and concrete.

'Jessica!'

Samson! The rich resonance of his beautiful voice could not be mistaken for any other. He was at the foot of the steps which led down to the lowest terrace, where he had obviously made use of the sunken swimming-pool. A towel was slung around his neck and moisture still clung to his powerful body...naked, except for a brief pair of swimming-trunks.

'Wait for me!' he commanded, and bounded up the steps, surprisingly light on his feet for so big a man.

Jessica could not help but notice that there was not an ounce of fat on him. He was superbly proportioned within his huge frame, and all impressive flesh and muscle. His hair shone a brilliant red-gold and even his grin seemed full of sunlight.

'Having a swim first thing in the morning is a great way to start the day,' he declared as he reached her. 'How about joining me tomorrow?'

'I'm afraid I'm not much of a swimmer,' she demurred, wary of being too friendly with him. 'I was brought up in Broken Hill, and while that's not exactly the outback, it's a long way from water.'

He laughed, his eyes skipping over her with a warm, appreciative twinkle. 'All the more reason to enjoy it now. Don't worry, Jessica. I won't let you drown.' He took her arm in a gently persuasive manner. 'Come and have breakfast with me.'

'No. Thank you, I'm just on my way to work,' she said quickly. 'I had my breakfast some time ago.'

'Then I'll show you to the library.'

Clearly he was intent on having her company and Jessica could not see how to detach herself from him politely. After all, he was her employer's brother. She accompanied him inside, guardedly answering the questions he asked about herself. However, when he led her into the library, Jessica stood stock-still in amazement and just shook her head.

For a private library this had to be unique. Floor-to-ceiling bookcases were filled with beautifully bound books. There was a computer for storing or drawing files as well as a microfiche, a film reader, map-cases, filing cabinets, several wide desks for working on, and a number of comfortable leather chairs. A spiral staircase apparently led up to another floor and Samson provided the answer even before the question formed in her mind.

'To the observatory on the roof. Dad had it built so he could study the stars as the early navigators did.'

He said it as if it was the simplest thing in the world to add an observatory to all the other wonders that comprised Pillatoro. And it probably was to him. 'It's like a dream...to work in a place like this,' Jessica observed, moving over to the nearest desk and trailing her fingers along the polished edge, touching wood in an attempt to reinforce its reality.

Sam followed her and picked up her hand, pressing it lightly to refocus her attention on him. She shrank back a little, but he held on and his serious expression denied any suggestion of over-familiarity. 'Jessica, I hope you will be happy working here. This project of my father's...' He frowned and gave a little shake of his head. 'It's an obsession with Gideon. I hope...'

The door opened and Gideon stepped into the library. The relaxed air with which he had entered the room lasted barely a second. Jessica was instantly and acutely aware of what he saw... Samson in his flagrant bareness, turned so intently towards her, holding her hand. A hot wave of embarrassment flooded up her neck.

'Good morning,' he said with remote formality.

'Ah, there you are, Gideon,' Sam said, without the slightest suggestion that he had been interrupted in any way. He smiled at Jessica and released her hand. 'I'll see you tonight at dinner, if not before.' Then he was walking towards the door. 'I'll let you have Jessica during work hours, Gideon, but then she's mine,' he declared breezily on his way out.

The silence he left behind screamed with tension. For several moments Gideon did not move or speak, and despite all Jessica's resolutions she was powerless to do anything but stare back at him, wishing fiercely that she had been alone when he had entered the room.

He was dressed more casually this morning, but the smartly tailored trousers and open-necked shirt did not soften the austere reserve of the man. He showed no interest whatsoever in her appearance. He seemed to look straight through her, almost as if she weren't there. Then, with a curt gesture towards the technical equipment he began to speak.

'Doris Mavin, your secretary, will be here shortly. She'll show you the filing and index systems. If you need any other equipment for what you have to do, please inform me. Doris worked with my father and will supply you with all his notes and maps.'

With barely a pause, Gideon proceeded to outline his father's theory. It was a detailed, comprehensive and difficult summary, and it took a tremendous effort of will for Jessica to follow it. She reminded herself that her job could be at stake, yet Gideon's physical presence and the sharp memory of the emotional confusion he had stirred last night combined to destroy the professional detachment she should have been exercising.

Not by a look or a gesture was there even the slightest recollection of their meeting on the balcony. It was as if it had never happened. Yet Jessica found her gaze wavering to his mouth over and over again as it formed word after word...the rather thin upper lip, the fuller lower one...and the memory of his kiss kept throbbing through her mind.

Gideon suddenly stopped talking. With a guilty start Jessica glanced up to find a frown of irritation directed at her. Panic squeezed her heart. Had he been aware of her lapse in concentration? The dark, probing eyes seemed to be reassessing her as he resumed speaking.

'I'll give you a list of the people my father employed. Use any or all of them. Looking for a needle in a haystack will be child's play compared to this. The answers do not lie in indexes.' He paused, then with slow deliberation, added, 'Do you think you are fully competent, or would you rather not lay your reputation on the line?'

Pride in her abilities gave her the necessary courage to answer him. 'I can organise and do the research for you. I still can't promise that you'll get the answer you want.'

His face tightened into stony command. 'When the proof has been found, all my father's papers will be printed by the Cavilha Foundation. It will serve as one small monument to his...his perception and dedication and tenacity.'

The hint of barely controlled passion in those last words made Jessica very uneasy. No matter what

Gideon wanted, nor how much he wanted it, she knew that she could not compromise her professional integrity; yet at this moment she couldn't find the will to fight him. There was time enough for that argument after she had evaluated his father's work.

Then suddenly the cold reserve in which he had wrapped himself snapped open and his eyes caught hers in urgent demand. 'Jessica... I want that proof!'

Jessica was staggered by the pain she sensed in him, a deep writhing of the soul that was in quest of a peace he couldn't find. Without thinking, on sheer instinctive impulse, she reached out and softly touched his arm. 'I will do everything I possibly can.'

The door was pushed open again, breaking the intimate mood of the moment, much to Jessica's acute frustration. For the first time Gideon Cavilha had revealed something of himself that she had sensed was terribly important, yet she hadn't had time to understand it. And the austere mask of authority had settled back on to his face as a pleasant-faced woman in her mid-fifties entered the library.

'Good morning, Mr Gideon,' she said, and her gaze shifted curiously to Jessica.

Gideon quickly introduced her as Doris Mavin, the secretary who was to be Jessica's personal assistant. He left them shortly afterwards, and his departure gave Jessica a curiously hollow feeling of disappointment. It was difficult to put the enigma that was Gideon Cavilha out of her mind, but the wealth of historical material that Doris produced for her gradually claimed her full attention.

They worked together in close harmony until they were interrupted at one o'clock by a maid who brought them a lunch tray. Beautifully arranged salads and fresh bread rolls were set out for them and Doris grinned at Jessica as the door shut behind the maid.

'One of the perks of working at Pillatoro. The Cavilhas expect the best, but they treat you well. Fantastic place, isn't it?' she added as they set themselves to eat lunch.

'It certainly is,' Jessica agreed with feeling.

Doris eyed her curiously. 'You really surprised me this morning. I was expecting Mr Gideon to hire a man, and someone older.'

A little smile of irony curved Jessica's mouth. 'He surprised me, too. But I hope I can satisfy his requirements,' she added matter-of-factly, not wanting to arouse Doris's curiosity further. 'How long have you been working here?'

The answer to that took up the rest of the lunch-hour. The afternoon sped by as Jessica became more and more absorbed in the brilliant mind of Richard Cavilha as revealed in the legacy of his notes. Doris packed up and left at five o'clock, but it was almost six before Jessica finally dragged herself away from her desk. It had been a long day and she wanted to freshen up before facing Samson and Gideon Cavilha at dinner.

However, as she stepped out into the hallway, the front door opened to admit a beautiful young girl, closely followed by Gideon, who slid his arm around the girl's shoulders in an affectionate manner which sent a cold chill through Jessica's heart. His expression of soft indulgence still lingered on his face as he caught sight of Jessica.

'I don't expect you to work this late, Jessica.'

'I was interested,' she returned evenly, hiding the foolish vulnerability that his presence evoked in her.

Whether her answer pleased him or not she could not tell. His arm dropped from the girl's shoulders as he steered her forward. She looked to be still in her teens, but she had the innate poise of someone older. Her lovely face was lit by large, hazel eyes which were almost luminous. A halo of black curls highlighted the honey-tan of her skin, which was shown off to even greater advantage by a dress boldly splashed with pink, green and orange flowers. She was petite, her head barely reaching to Gideon's shoulder, but her body was all woman, every line a flowing curve in beautiful proportion.

'Bernadette, I'd like you to meet Jessica Trelawney, who's come here to complete my father's work,' Gideon stated matter-of-factly. 'And this is Bernadette Adriani, Jessica, a very close friend of the family who will be dining with us tonight.'

Bernadette shot him a happy look as she offered her hand to Jessica. Her smile showed small, even white teeth. 'I'm very pleased to meet you, Jessica,' she said in a soft, musical voice which projected guileless sincerity.

Her appeal was irresistible and Jessica found herself accepting her hand and smiling back automatically.

Bernadette's eyes suddenly twinkled with mischief. 'You mustn't let Gideon browbeat you, you know. He's a terrible tyrant and always has been.'

Jessica darted an apprehensive look at Gideon, but he simply smiled at Bernadette. An amused smile. 'Is that the thanks I get for inviting you here? Undermining my authority as soon as you get into the house?'

Bernadette laughed and tucked her arm around his. 'Oh, you can't be stern tonight, Gideon. It's so marvellous to be at Pillatoro again. And Sam is home.'

Even his eyes smiled. 'Obviously I mustn't argue with that. We'll go and find Sam and you can say hello to him too.' The smile was still in place as his gaze lifted again. 'Please excuse us, Jessica. We'll be having drinks in the small lounge before dinner. Please join us when you're ready. We'll be dining at seven-thirty.'

He swept Bernadette off without waiting for an answer and Jessica stared after them, feeling hopelessly at odds with herself. Every scrap of common sense told her that it was far better if Gideon Cavilha kept his personal relationships to people of his own kind and left her strictly alone, except in so far as the job was concerned.

After all, the job was very important to her, critical in her circumstances. Hadn't Rex taught her a savage enough lesson about the consequences of becoming emotionally involved with the man who held the whip-hand over one's career?

In any event, Bernadette Adriani had come at Gideon's invitation, and his manner to the beautiful girl certainly spelled out where his affections lay. Jessica knew she should feel relieved, yet a dull heaviness sat on her heart as she walked to her room.

There was no denying she felt strongly attracted to Gideon Cavilha. Far too strongly. And she didn't understand it at all. Only three weeks ago she had been broken-hearted over Rex, and yet Gideon Cavilha had the power to stir her in a far deeper sense than Rex had ever done.

Jessica stripped off her clothes and took a long, soothing shower. She recalled Bernadette's vibrant silk dress, and knew there was nothing in her own wardrobe that could compete with it. Not that she had the kind of looks that could wear such colours anyway, Jessica thought wryly, but she felt particularly colourless tonight.

She hesitated for a long time over her choice of dress, finally picking out her old favourite. It had been her graduation dress, the obligatory white, but it was well cut and the simplicity of its style suited her tall, slim figure. The softly gathered blouson top ended in a plaited belt with string ties, and the circular skirt was graceful.

Jessica had not intended undoing her hair, and she told herself she was stupid to do so even as her fingers removed the pins, yet as she brushed it into a long, smooth curtain she could not banish the memory of Gideon's hand stroking it that dreadful afternoon in Rex's office. She wanted him to be attracted to her. Despite all the tenets of common sense, that was more necessary to her than anything else.

However, when Mrs Price showed her into the small lounge-room, it was not Gideon who reacted to her appearance. Samson rose to his feet, his eyes alight with admiration, his voice rich with appreciation.

'You're just like a Renaissance painting come to life! I thought you lovely last night, Jessica, but now I stand transfixed. You are exquisite.'

Jessica was tongue-tied. She had thought so exclusively of Gideon, that she had completely forgotten Samson's admiration of her and his desire for her company. His outburst now came as an unwelcome shock. He stepped forward, hands outstretched to take hers and draw her into the room, and there was nothing she could do to evade him. He was so big he blotted out any line of vision to Gideon and Bernadette.

He took her arm in a courtly manner and steered her to an armchair. 'Now, what can I get you to drink? It will be my pleasure to serve you with anything you want.'

It seemed hopelessly trite to ask for a dry sherry. Jessica felt her cheeks burning with embarrassment and she could not bring herself to look at Gideon. Out of the corner of her eye she saw him lean over from the adjacent chair and take Bernadette's hand, giving it a light squeeze.

The girl flicked a grateful glance at Gideon, who squeezed her hand again in gentle reassurance. There was a rapport between them that Jessica fiercely envied. She wanted Gideon to touch her like that, look at her in the same soft way as he looked at Bernadette, and she knew she was being totally irrational.

Sam handed her a glass of sherry, his face still showing open admiration. 'With eyes as blue as yours, Jessica, you must love the sea as I do. Have you ever been sailing?'

'No,' she answered quietly.

'Ah, there's nothing like it!' Sam said with authority, subsiding in the chair next to hers. 'A calm night and star-studded waters; or even better is a howling storm with the rigging shrieking like a banshee, the boat bucking against the waves, and the wildness of the elements gone berserk. Of all things, I like controlling that best.' His grin was sublime happiness. 'I'll take you out in the boat tomorrow. You'll love it.'

'I thought...' Bernadette started, then bit her lips. Her long lashes swept down, veiling whatever thoughts she had.

Gideon shot a dark look of exasperation at his brother. 'You asked Bernadette to go with you, Sam,' he reminded him tersely.

Jessica tried to extricate herself from the invitation. 'I don't think...'

Sam didn't let her finish. 'Well, of course Bernadette is coming. Hasn't she always been my favourite crew?' He grinned at the girl who flushed with pleasure. 'You don't mind if Jessica comes too, do you, Bernadette?' he demanded cheerfully.

Bernadette flashed Jessica an oddly moving look of appeal. 'No, of course not. If you don't mind my being there, Jessica.'

'There! That's settled!' Sam declared in triumphant satisfaction.

Gideon was about to say more when Bernadette's fingers closed over his wrist. She smiled at Jessica. 'Sam's right. You'll enjoy it, Jessica. Please come.'

There were so many confusing cross-currents alive in the room that Jessica instinctively retreated from the situation. 'Thank you. It's very kind of

you both, but I'd really prefer to stay here. I want
to get a full grasp of the project as soon as possible.'

'Tomorrow is Saturday. You're entitled to the day
off,' Samson argued.

She felt intensely awkward about refusing him
when he was obviously so eager for her company,
but she did not want to be pushed into anything,
particularly not when she understood so little about
Pillatoro and the people involved with it. 'Perhaps
another time, Sam,' she said, not wanting to offend
him.

To her great relief a maid appeared at the door
and announced that dinner would shortly be served.
Samson looked disappointed, but he immediately
climbed to his feet and offered Jessica his arm. He
really was larger than life, Jessica reflected as he
led her into the dining-room.

The table was of a size that could seat six or eight
people comfortably. The mirrorlike finish of the
polished cedar reflected the crystal glasses and the
silver cutlery of the four place-settings. The chairs
were high-backed and upholstered in a flaming
scarlet velvet. Their stunning richness and craftsmanship were typical of the many splendours within
the walls of Pillatoro. Mrs Price had shown Jessica
the adjoining banquet-room where at least two
dozen people could be seated in a similarly magnificent setting.

But tonight Jessica took no joy in her surroundings. Sam dominated the conversation with
a natural exuberance which did not recognise that
anyone was in less good spirits than himself. Jessica
could not enjoy being the focus of his attention.
While Samson Cavilha was immensely likeable, she

was too conscious that he was attracted to her, and she felt uncomfortable about it.

Bernadette grew quieter and quieter, only brightening when Gideon drew some remark from her, which he did less and less. Sam did not seem to notice the strained atmosphere but Jessica was all too aware of it. As soon as dinner was over she excused herself from the table, quietly but firmly refusing to accept any of Sam's protests at her early departure.

Gideon courteously held the door open for her. 'Thank you,' she whispered as she passed by him, too conscious of his stern demeanour to lift her gaze to his.

'Thank you, Jessica.'

The soft benediction floated after her and for a moment her step faltered. Why was he thanking her? she asked herself. She shook her head and walked on, not understanding anything about Gideon Cavilha. She fiercely wished that he did not affect her so deeply. His manner and words had shown all too clearly that Bernadette had his first consideration.

Yet there was comfort in Luisa's room. It seemed to welcome Jessica and soothe her troubled spirits. She did feel at home in it, just as Gideon had surmised, and the strange part was, Jessica no longer wanted to question why he had given it to her. She didn't care as long as she could stay here.

CHAPTER FIVE

JESSICA felt him watching her. Even though she told herself that she had to be imagining it, her gaze lifted from the notes on her desk and swept the library. Gideon Cavilha stood at the far end of the room, propped against the doorway which led to his offices, and he had been watching her. Was still watching her.

A slight smile curved his mouth as he straightened and began to walk towards her. 'I don't expect you to work at weekends, Jessica.'

'It interests me,' she defended.

'And blocks out other thoughts,' he said softly.

The perceptive comment struck deep. She felt a flush rising to her cheeks and tore her gaze from his, afraid that he might see how she thought of him.

He reached her desk, leaned over and shut the folder of notes. 'I'll show you around Pillatoro.'

It was a command more than an invitation and Jessica bridled at his autocratic manner. It was bad enough that he dominated her thoughts. It would be extremely foolish of her to let him order her actions.

The hand on her desk turned up in a gesture of appeal. 'Don't you want to see it all?'

His voice asked the question, but there was an undertone that told her he already knew the answer. Pillatoro fascinated her. Gideon Cavilha fascinated her. And despite where it might lead, she could not resist the temptation he was holding out to her.

She glanced up into the eyes that saw too much and nodded. 'Thank you. I would like that.'

He held her chair back as she stood up and every nerve in Jessica's body vibrated at his closeness, but he did not touch her. Nor did he touch her as he accompanied her out of the library. Jessica paused in the entrance hallway and looked up at the stained-glass window that sprinkled them with soft pools of colour in the afternoon sunshine.

'The picture in the glass... I know it's a religious scene, but who is the saint?'

'Saint Jude,' Gideon answered. 'He is known as the hope of the hopeless, the only one who can help when all else fails. He graces that wall to remind all the Cavilhas who live here that nothing is impossible.'

The building and the grounds were proof of that, Jessica thought, but she made no comment.

'To Rafael and Luisa, it was the cornerstone on which Pillatoro was built,' Gideon continued. 'Rafael had to leave Portugal, because he was too poor, too socially inferior for Luisa's parents to permit her to marry him. He came to Australia and tried his hand at the gold diggings—the hope of the hopeless. He endured the greatest hardships and privations and was near death several times. For eight long years he kept praying to Saint Jude, asking him to plead his cause with God, in the name of love. Finally he discovered gold at Maryborough, in Victoria, in 1859. It was a major strike.'

'So it was gold that started it,' Jessica murmured, thinking of the wealth that had been needed to build this huge complex.

'No.'

Jessica looked up at him in surprise and once again was caught by his dark, compelling gaze. 'It was love, Jessica. Blind, unreasoning love that overrode time and circumstances.'

Jessica's heart skipped a beat. She felt he was asking her if she had loved like that, and suddenly she knew she hadn't.

'Luisa waited for Rafael, even though she did not know whether he was dead or alive. Despite all the pressure from her family, she refused to marry any other. I believe she would have waited for him all her life.'

Gideon paused, lending a quiet emphasis to that point, then added, 'When Rafael returned to Portugal for her, she cut all her ties with her family and came back to Australia with him. They built Pillatoro together.'

Jessica was intensely moved by the story. 'They must have loved each other very deeply,' she said with a heavy sigh, thinking how shallow her affair with Rex had been.

'All Cavilhas love deeply,' Gideon murmured, and there was a shade of pain in his voice.

He turned towards the entrance doors and Jessica fell into step beside him, fiercely wishing that he would reveal more of himself to her. Whenever she had felt close to him he had always quickly retreated into a dark world of his own where she could not follow.

'It must have taken many years to build,' she remarked, wanting him to keep talking.

'Yes. It was built to last for ever. Unfortunately, our family may not last that long,' he said with a touch of bitter irony.

'Why do you say that?' Jessica asked curiously.

He shrugged. 'Each generation has been dogged by tragedy.'

They walked down to the courtyard and Gideon gestured towards the lion gateway. They strolled out to the gardens which Jessica had only seen by moonlight when she arrived. Gideon pointed out the sections planted by the various generations and told her the Cavilha story.

It was a sad tale of young men killed in the many wars that had plagued mankind, children lost to sickness, women widowed before even bearing children to their husbands. But it was also a story of endurance, of determined building towards a better life.

Jessica was enthralled by their history, and deeply moved by it, so moved that she felt personally involved with every member of the family who had lived and died here. And running through the whole story was Pillatoro, which was more than a home. It was a monument to the lives of the people it had sheltered and nurtured, and the memories of them were housed within its walls, never forgotten.

They walked up through the servants' quarters and along the colonnaded balcony to the parapet beyond the ballroom. Gideon paused there, leaning on the stone wall which topped the cliff-face and gazing out at the white yacht that was ploughing through the waves towards safe harbour.

'There are only Sam and I left of the line that Rafael and Luisa began,' he remarked.

Jessica joined him at the wall, although the height of the cliff made her feel slightly nervous. 'But you're both young enough to marry and have children,' she said artlessly, only wanting this grand tradition to continue.

His face seemed to tighten. 'I hope Sam will marry soon.'

Was he warning her off Sam, telling her not to take any encouragement from his admiration? And why should he speak only of Sam marrying and not of himself? She wanted to ask him, but there was something forbidding about his stern profile that stopped her.

The image of Bernadette floated into her mind and she stared out at the yacht, wondering if Gideon was thinking of the beautiful young girl who was sailing on it. She suddenly felt very empty and miserable. The breeze from the ocean was cool, but it was a chill in her heart that made her shiver.

She had thought Gideon was no longer aware of her presence, but he instantly lifted an arm and curled it around her shoulders. 'You're cold,' he murmured, hugging her to the warmth of his body.

Her pulse went crazy. Jessica's heart seemed to be catapulting around her chest. Did he intend to kiss her again? She looked up at him shyly, but she could not read his countenance. Everywhere his body touched hers, her skin was prickling with a vibrant awareness. Never had she had such an intense physical reaction to anyone, not even Rex. She tried to control it, keeping absolutely still, not éven breathing, mortified at the thought that he might realise what his touch was doing to her.

She tried to reason herself out of it. She had not been affected like this when Gideon had held her that day in Rex's office. Why was this happening now? What had changed? And her mind answered that everything had changed since she had come to Pillatoro, since she had met Gideon Cavilha, since he had kissed her. It was unreasonable, but she suddenly knew that she wanted him. She wanted, quite desperately, to be part of him and all he stood for.

His fingers lightly caressed her upper arm and it was all she could do not to turn and press herself against him. 'We'll go and get you a cardigan,' he suggested matter-of-factly.

'No, I ... I'm not really cold,' Jessica demurred quickly, not wanting to move out of the circle of his arm.

Gideon turned slightly towards her, a slight smile curving his mouth. 'Would you like to walk down to the bay and meet Sam and Bernadette?'

Her mind screamed rejection. She couldn't face seeing Gideon and Bernadette together... not now while she was still reeling from the revelation of her own feelings. 'Please excuse me,' she said stiffly, and forced herself to draw away from him. 'I'll go back to the library, if you don't mind.'

He frowned at her, eyes sharply probing her defences. 'Does Sam...?' He paused and began again. 'Some people find Sam rather overwhelming, but he has the gentlest heart in the whole world. You have no need to be wary of him, Jessica.'

'I'm not,' she denied swiftly, but she found the assurance very confusing. Was friendship with Sam all right as long as she didn't get above herself?

Gideon nodded, although he didn't look fully satisfied. 'Your time's your own outside work hours. Do as you please,' he murmured, releasing her from his presence.

Jessica went to the library. She shut the door behind her but she didn't go back to her desk. She knew she couldn't concentrate on work. Her mind was in turmoil. She thought of her relationship with Rex and realised that it had been nothing but an infatuation on her part, an infatuation that Rex had manipulated for his own ends.

She had been so flattered when the celebrated Professor Anderson had begun to take notice of her. She had thought he was the most knowledgeable, cultured man alive. In a way she had hero-worshipped him, but he was a fallen idol now. It mortified her to remember how malleable she had been, doing all she could to please him, to win his favour.

He had never touched her soul as Gideon Cavilha did. Jessica wondered how she was going to hide what she felt on a continuing day-to-day basis. Somehow she would have to control her reaction to Gideon because she didn't want to leave Pillatoro.

When she felt sure that Gideon would have left the parapet to go down to the bay, Jessica left the library and wandered outside again. Without even thinking of where she was going or what she would do, she turned down the flight of steps which led to the terrace below the bedroom wing.

For a little while she gazed unseeingly at the swimming-pool set in its bed of rock, then kept wandering. She passed changing-rooms, a spa and sauna, a gymnasium, hobby-rooms; barely noting their existence. She did not even know why she entered the schoolroom, except perhaps it was the last of the line and she couldn't think where else to go.

She closed the door behind her and leaned against it. Only gradually did her gaze focus on the room. It was quaint and old-fashioned, in some ways reminiscent of a doll's house. The desks had turn-up seats and the blackboard stood on a three-legged stand. Low casement windows provided seats on which were piled gaily coloured cushions, inviting young readers to snuggle up with a book. There were shelves loaded with educational puzzles and toys, and cupboards undoubtedly full of books and paints and all the other needs of a schoolroom.

It was the wall behind the blackboard which drew Jessica's full attention. It was decorated with framed pictures, all done by childish hands, and Jessica walked over to examine them more closely. There were nearly forty of them, all dated and signed, and since the dates ran from 1871 onwards, Jessica surmised that every child taught in this room had contributed one picture to be hung on this wall. Some of the names she recognised as those that Gideon had mentioned.

She dropped to her knees to look at the last two, expecting them to be signed by Gideon and Samson. But the names printed on them were Benjamin and Nicholas, and they were dated 1982. Jessica frowned over the date.

Her gaze slid back a painting: Samson—1960.
The picture was of a great windjammer sailing
through tempestuous seas. Jessica smiled over it,
recalling Samson's enthusiasm for sailing in all
weathers. Then there was Gideon's—1958, a man
on top of a mountain with his arms reaching up to
the sky. It seemed that even as a child he had the
instinct of a conqueror.

But who were Benjamin and Nicholas? Jessica
frowned over the most recent paintings. Benjamin's was of a boy riding a horse bareback.
Nicholas had painted trees and flowers. Whose
children were they? Gideon had not mentioned
having had a sister. Jessica's gaze swept back to the
picture beyond Gideon's. Rachel—1927. Not a
sister. Jessica puzzled over the mystery for a while
and then shrugged it off. It was not the past she
should be worrying about, but the present.

She had to learn to cope with her reaction to
Gideon. She walked outside and over to the fur-
thermost corner of the terrace beyond the pool. Her
gaze swept back over all she could see of Pillatoro.
It had wound around her heart, just as Gideon
Cavilha had.

'Jessica! There you are!' The booming voice of
Samson Cavilha hailed her from the balcony. He
came barging down the steps and across the terrace,
his face beaming with the pleasure of seeing her.
No darkness about Samson Cavilha, Jessica
thought in some relief. He showed exactly what he
felt, and his bright personality was a happy con-
trast to his brother's.

'You should have come with us. It was a marvellous day for sailing,' he enthused.

Jessica had to smile. 'I saw the yacht coming in. It looked beautiful.'

'Best thing I ever bought. Come with me to-morrow, Jessica.'

She shook her head. 'Maybe next weekend.' When she had got herself in hand. If she could manage that.

'You haven't been working all day?' Sam accused in some frustration.

'No. As a matter of fact, I've just been exploring the schoolroom.' The question that had tantalised her mind slid off her tongue. 'I was wondering who Nicholas and Benjamin were, Sam.'

No sooner were the words out than Jessica wished she had kept her curiosity to herself. Sam's face expressed an agony of heart which was still fresh in his memory. They were long, nerve-prickling moments before he brought himself to answer her and his voice carried a heavy load of grief.

'They were Gideon's children. You might remember the Ash Wednesday bushfires that left so much of Victoria and South Australia devastated a couple of years ago. Almost a hundred people were burnt to death. Our father, Gideon's wife, Alison, and his two sons were among them.'

'No!' Jessica whispered, horror squeezing her heart. She had seen the devastation of the Ash Wednesday bushfires on television...so many lives, homes and properties destroyed...the appalling toll had moved her to tears then, but the dreadful loss suffered by Gideon...Gideon and Sam...it was far beyond anything she had suffered.

'How terrible,' she breathed, suddenly understanding the pain she had seen in Gideon's eyes.

'It was worse than that, Jessica.' Sam shook his head, drew in a deep breath and continued. 'Alison had always loved horses and Gideon bought her a stud farm as an interest. She and Dad had taken the two boys down there for a week. The week of the fires, as it turned out. Gideon was in Melbourne when he heard that the farm was under threat by the bushfire. He drove out immediately and ran into a road blockade seven kilometres from the farm. They wouldn't let him pass. Said it was too late. They tried to stop him, but no one can stop Gideon. He went in on foot. It was an inferno, trees exploding from the heat...'

His voice trailed off, the horror of the memory etched on his face. Jessica reached out and touched his arm in mute sympathy. 'You don't have to tell me any more, Sam. I'm sorry I asked. I didn't think...didn't imagine...'

He covered her hand with his own and gave her a sad smile. 'No. It's better that I explain. Gideon can't put it behind him and sometimes...' He heaved a rueful sigh. 'It's best that you know what drives him. Particularly since you're working on this project. He's obsessed with it.'

'What has the project to do with this?' Jessica asked in bewilderment.

'Let me finish and you'll see. I got to the blockade about twenty minutes after Gideon. I'd flown down from Sydney, having heard the news flashes about the fires. I went after Gideon and found him about two kilometres short of the homestead. He was unconscious from the smoke and already badly burnt from where he had fallen. I carried him out...'

Carried him! For five kilometres of burning bush! Only a man of Samson's strength could have done it, Jessica thought in awe.

'...I handed Gideon over to ambulancemen then went back in for Alison and the children. I thought Dad would have got them somewhere safe. The fire had swept on. The homestead was rubble, but no one had been in it. I found them huddled together in a group, half-way to the dam which might have saved their lives. A burning tree had fallen across their path and they'd been incinerated where they stood.'

Sam shook his head and tears glittered in his eyes. 'Thank God Gideon was spared that sight. I'll never forget it as long as I live... Dad's arms stretched around them all, trying to...' He choked and fell silent.

'Oh, Sam,' Jessica breathed in heartfelt sympathy. He was a great man, with a truly great heart, and without the slightest hesitation she stepped forward and put her arms around him, wanting only to give comfort for the traumatic memory she had so unwittingly recalled.

Ironically enough he patted her back as if she were the one who needed comfort. 'Jessica,' he murmured. 'It's not so bad for me. It's Gideon who's scarred. Not so much physically, but...' His huge chest rose and fell in another sigh. 'I wish he'd talk about it. Let it out in the open. But that's not his way.'

No. That's the dark world he keeps inside him, Jessica thought sadly. She drew back from Sam's gentle embrace to look up at him, needing more answers. 'And the project?' she prompted, although her memory was already supplying the answer...a monument. That's what Gideon had said.

'It's the only thing left for him to do for any of them,' Sam replied. 'Except for keeping Pillatoro going. I leave that to Gideon because it keeps him occupied. It's a reason for living.'

Work...to keep other thoughts blocked out. She understood so much now...the compassion he had shown her that day in Rex's office...the passionate need to finish his father's work...the way his life was bound up with Pillatoro—his reason for being.

'Is the project going to work out right, Jessica?' Sam asked in sharp concern.

'I don't know yet, Sam,' she answered honestly, then remembered that she had left Richard Cavilha's notes on her desk. 'I must go up to the library and put your father's work away. I was looking at it earlier this afternoon and I left it out,' she explained. 'Thank you for telling me all this, Sam.'

His eyes softened as he gave her a gentle smile. 'You're part of Pillatoro now, Jessica. You had to know sooner or later.'

Part of it? Yes, she was, in some inextricable way, Jessica acknowledged. She smiled back. 'Thank you all the same. I must go now.'

He let her go. 'I'll see you at dinner,' he called after her.

'Yes,' she called back, but her mind was already fixed on Gideon, revolving all that had ever happened between them, fitting each piece into her new perspective of him. She wished there was something she could do to help him but there were no sure-fire answers, neither with the project, nor on any more personal level.

She thrust open the library door, her mind still feverish with thoughts. Her eyes glazed with shock as they caught sight of Gideon, his arms wrapped tightly around Bernadette who was clinging just as tightly to him. For one dreadful moment Gideon's gaze met Jessica's over Bernadette's head. Jessica did not stop to read whatever was to be read in those dark, fathomless eyes. She stepped back and closed the door, her heart pounding a thousand painful protests.

She had known about Bernadette, the sane half of her mind screamed. She forced herself to walk away. She walked to Luisa's room. She crawled on to the bed and hugged a pillow to her in a blind need for comfort. Gideon should not have given her this room. It was wrong, because she would never become his wife, never become the mistress of Pillatoro.

CHAPTER SIX

IT was impossible for Jessica to dislike Bernadette Adriani. The girl's natural beauty was matched by a lovely nature. Her fresh and unaffected personality carried a warmth that reached out to everyone in her company. She seemed to go out of her way to be nice to Jessica when they were all together at the dinner-table, and Jessica could only respond in like manner, even though every evidence of Bernadette's attractiveness added to her inner misery.

She turned to Sam for distraction and he joyfully grasped all the attention she gave him, delighted to expand on the sense of friendship she now felt with the big man. He was a marvellous raconteur with a knowledge of the world that was well outside Jessica's ken, and it was certainly no hardship to listen to him. Yet her awareness of Gideon never dropped for a moment. When he was not speaking to Bernadette, Jessica felt his eyes on her—watching. It was very disconcerting.

Bernadette did not stay beyond the weekend, which was some relief to Jessica. She plunged back into the evaluation of Richard Cavilha's theory with more dedication than ever, hoping that she could prove it right for Gideon.

Her days quickly divided into two types. There were the days that she saw Gideon, no matter how fleetingly; and there were the days she didn't. The latter always left her feeling that she had lost something vital to her life.

She saw Samson much more frequently and for longer periods than she saw Gideon, who regularly commuted to Sydney in his private helicopter. Sam told her that the head office for their various business interests was situated there, although their business connections stretched around the world. They owned forests for the production of paper, vineyards that exported wine, and there were other more complex lines of income.

Whenever Gideon did join Sam and Jessica for dinner, he said very little, seemingly content to listen to them talk. Nevertheless, Jessica was always conscious of his eyes on her, watching. As soon as she turned to him the intensity of that dark gaze was instantly hooded, as if denying any interest in her. Yet she felt his interest. It was terribly frustrating.

The Friday of her third weekend at Pillatoro was such a night. By the time Gideon left the dinner-table Jessica was in no mood for pretending pleasure in Sam's company, so she excused herself and went to her room. With Gideon so much on her mind she couldn't settle to anything. In the end she returned to the library. At least there she felt a sense of purpose that was related to Gideon.

It was after midnight when she heard the music. At first it was just an undercurrent of sound and only slowly did it filter through her perceptions until it had her full attention. There was a haunting quality to it, a depth of feeling that grabbed the heart.

It drew Jessica out of the library. As she closed the door behind her the volume of sound increased noticeably. It was coming from the room on the opposite side of the great hall, and although the thickness of the walls absorbed much of the sound, it was clear enough to captivate Jessica completely.

She was not an opera buff, but Rex had prided himself as one, and had owned a fine collection of recordings which he had played frequently. She had heard enough to recognise this music. It was Mussorgsky's 'Boris Godunov', but never had she heard a performance of this stature. The pure tonal quality of the great bass voice was riveting. It was so powerful, so emotional, so compelling, that Jessica's hand was on the doorknob to the room before she realised she might be an unwelcome intruder.

It was not a room she had ever entered, or been invited to enter, and it was a very late hour. But that great voice beckoned irresistibly and surely neither Sam nor Gideon would mind sharing it with her. Jessica twisted the knob and quietly pushed the door open.

Like every other room of Pillatoro, it stunned the mind with its magnificence. The carpet was a bold orange-gold, the walls papered in gold and black embossed velvet, the heavy curtains a tangerine silk. Exotic cushions, large enough to recline on, were strewn around the floor. The grand piano at one end of the room was dressed in black walnut to complement huge black leather chesterfields which formed a small auditorium at the other end.

Gideon was slumped in one of them, his eyes closed, his face rapt in tight concentration. As if he had somehow sensed the movement of the door, a frown of irritation drew sharp lines between his eyebrows and a narrowed gaze sliced to Jessica. Every nerve in her body tensed. He did not speak, but the frown disappeared and with a minimum of movement he gestured for her to come and sit next to him.

Jessica's relief was instantly followed by a surge of excitement. She shut the door quietly, tiptoed down the room and eased herself gently on to the soft, leather sofa, sitting at an angle that allowed her covertly to watch the effect of the music on Gideon. His eyes were closed again, his body thrown back in complete relaxation, absorbing every note of music and singing.

Slowly the opera moved to its dramatic conclusion with the two great bass arias in the death scene of Boris. Never before had Jessica heard such power and intensity of feeling conveyed by singing. The agony of mind, the bitterness of spirit, the alternations of hope and despair were elicited with a barbaric grandeur that surpassed the music. Jessica was totally overwhelmed by it, choked by the feelings aroused by what was not just a performance, but a creation of art on the highest scale.

The last notes echoed through the room, finally fading into silence. Gideon did not move to turn off the tape-player. He slowly opened his eyes and Jessica was startled to see the moistness of tears glittering in their darkness. She looked sharply away, embarrassed at having observed what a man as strong and as powerful as Gideon Cavilha would not want to have seen by anyone.

'Do you think I am without emotions, Jessica?' His voice was flat, steady, giving no indication of any emotional disturbance. But she knew what she had seen and he knew she had seen it.

Her embarrassment deepened. 'I...no...' She shook her head, hopelessly flustered until she found the courage to speak the truth as she knew it. 'You showed me on the day you hired me that you're a person of great compassion, but you're also the most controlled person I've ever met. I didn't expect it ... for you to show what you felt,' she finished in an awkward rush, darting an agitated glance at him.

He was not even looking at her. He seemed to have sunk into a brooding reverie. 'I'm tired. I'm tired of being what's expected of me,' he muttered, then slowly turned his gaze to her, a gleam of self-derision in the dark eyes. 'There are some things I feel very deeply. It seems to me I've spent all my life living up to expectations. But the role has worn thin, Jessica. I don't want to carry it any more. I want ...'

He paused and his expression changed, his eyes sharpening to an urgent probing. He leaned slightly towards her as his arm lifted and came to rest along the back of the chesterfield. The light stroke of his fingers on the back of her neck spread an instant tension through Jessica's body. It was the tension of anticipation, but the touch was abruptly withdrawn.

'Forgive me,' Gideon bit out, and pushed himself to his feet.

Jessica could have cried with frustration as he strode to the other end of the room. There was nothing to forgive. She didn't care about his relationship with Bernadette. She had wanted his touch. Wanted more than his touch. She wondered if she should move too, but the hope that he might return to the sofa kept her still.

He opened a cupboard, flicked a number of switches, then closed the doors to the bank of hi-fi equipment that had been briefly revealed. He turned back to Jessica, but seemed to speak more to himself than to her.

'Sam is more than my brother. I owe him everything I have left, so I may be biased. But to my mind, that performance is the equal of anything I've ever heard. It puts Sam on a level with Chaliapin, Christoff and Ghiaurov as one of the greatest basses of all time.'

It took a second to register and even then Jessica was incredulous. 'That was Sam singing?'

Surprise raised Gideon's eyebrows. 'You didn't know?'

She looked her puzzlement. 'I'm sure I should have known. Such a great voice ...'

Gideon interrupted her. 'Have you ever heard of Rebecca Magee?'

Jessica slowly shook her head. The name was vaguely familiar, but she could not place it. Gideon gestured towards a large portrait on the wall behind the piano. The woman depicted was striking in a theatrical sense. Flaming red hair billowed around a face which was too strong to be called pretty, yet it held that quality of composure and inner serenity that was almost beautiful.

'She was my mother. Our mother,' he corrected with a note of poignant sadness. 'After the Second World War she was the leading mezzo at Covent Garden. My father met her and fell in love. He wanted to marry her. It was a terrible decision she had to make. The opera houses of Europe are a long way from Australia. She had to choose between her love for my father and her lifelong love of singing.'

A ghost of a smile flitted over Gideon's mouth. 'Eventually my father persuaded her to come here for a short holiday. She never left. She never continued her career. She married my father. We all loved her... so very much. It seemed to us that the heart went out of Pillatoro when she died.'

He paused and seemed to recollect himself with an effort, then continued in a matter-of-fact tone. 'So, Sam sings as...'

'Samson Magee,' Jessica supplied softly.

'Yes. To honour her.'

It all fell into place. Samson Magee was an international star. Jessica had even seen one of his performances at the Sydney Opera House, but his hair and beard had been dyed grey and he had played the role of an old man.

'I've been such a fool not to have recognised him,' she muttered, lifting an apologetic gaze to Gideon. 'Even with his name changed, his voice was so obviously trained.'

'It doesn't matter. The last thing Sam wants is adulation,' Gideon commented drily.

He walked back to her and drew Jessica to her feet in the commanding manner that was so natural to him. His hands fell lightly around her waist. She tried to stay relaxed, tried to quell the excitement pumping through her heart. It was impossible. She looked up expectantly, but his eyes held a dark intensity that denied any spark of desire for her. Whatever was on his mind was hidden behind an opaque shield of hard watchfulness.

'Sam admires you very much.'

The soft statement held a strained note which implied a question, but Jessica didn't know what answer he was looking for. 'And I admire him,' she said in some confusion of mind.

'Before or after you realised who he was?'

The cynical thrust of the question brought an angry flush to Jessica's cheeks. 'Of course I admire him as a truly great artist. Who wouldn't?' she said defensively. 'But I've liked him as a person from the start. And admired his...his exuberant personality.'

The tension emanating from Gideon coiled around her, almost stifling her breath. Her chest felt constricted and her heart seemed to be pounding in her ears. She did not understand what he wanted of her, but he held her bound to him by the compelling demand in his eyes.

'Would you ever love him?'

Love Samson? For a moment the thought filled her mind, coloured by the larger-than-life ebullience that was Sam. 'Yes,' she said sincerely. 'As a marvellous friend or as a brother, but if you mean as a...a man, no, I never would,' she answered with absolute certainty.

There was no relaxation of tension but when Gideon spoke again his voice was less controlled, and his words throbbed with deep emotion. 'Sam and I may be very different, but there is nothing I wouldn't do for him. Nothing!'

Jessica did not doubt it. Gideon's feeling for his family had already been amply demonstrated. It seemed to her it was the only point of vulnerability he possessed and it gave him a humanity which made him even more attractive. 'I understand that,' she murmured.

'Do you, Jessica? Do you really understand?' His eyes bored into hers. The pressure of his hands on her waist increased. 'What if Sam asked you to marry him? Would you ever say yes?'

Marry! Was he so worried about any potential relationship she might have with Sam? That Gideon should even advance such an idea stunned her for a moment, but her answer was unequivocal. 'No.'

'Can you be sure of that, Jessica?'

'Yes,' she whispered, barely able to find breath, so sharply affected was she by the vibrant tension of his body so close to hers.

Couldn't he see that her life was bound up with his? she thought wildly. Hadn't he known it from the moment he had kissed her? Couldn't he feel what was so evident to her? And for a moment, just a fleeting moment, the craving want in her soul seemed to be reflected in his eyes.

Her heart cramped into a tight ball. She almost threw herself against him, but in the instant before that impulse would have condemned her Gideon released her, and the intimacy that had throbbed so briefly between them was broken by his harsh, discordant laugh.

'Can we ever be sure of anything?' he grated as he turned away.

Jessica could make no answer. She was so severely shaken it was all she could do to keep standing there.

Gideon paced a few steps away from her, then threw her a travesty of a smile. 'You shouldn't have walked in here tonight. You caught me at a bad time. It's a pity the real world doesn't cater for dreams, but God knows I've had my fill of dreams turned to ashes. And I guess you have too, if I'm not mistaken,' he added more gently.

Still Jessica could not speak, although her heart went out to him as he spoke obliquely of the grief that still haunted him. Her own short grief over Rex shamed her when measured against Gideon's suffering.

He paced a few more steps, his face darkly brooding. Then he swung on her with an air of reluctant decision. 'There's something I should tell you. I meant to mention it at dinner-time but you seemed quite happy with Sam, and I...' He gave a slight shake of his head. 'It's not my decision.'

His eyes stabbed at her across the space he had made. 'There's a group of people from the Cultural and Heritage Commission coming here tomorrow. Ostensibly to assess Pillatoro for its historical value. Professor Anderson is one of them.'

Jessica felt faint. The way Gideon was watching her...did he know what Rex had done to her? What she had done to herself by giving in to Rex? 'Do you need me here?' she asked, forcing herself to form the words.

'No. Their mission has nothing to do with my father's work. Your work.' He paused and seemed to choose his words carefully. 'I merely thought that since you and Professor Anderson were colleagues, you might want to be here to...speak to him.'

Jessica never wanted to see Rex again as long as she lived, but such a statement from her would be far too revealing. 'Any talk between Professor

Anderson and myself would be of no consequence,' she said flatly. 'I told Sam I would go sailing with him.'

Gideon's face relaxed. 'Then go sailing by all means. I'm sure Sam will see that you enjoy it.' His mouth thinned in distaste as he added, 'I'll deal with Professor Anderson.'

The oddly grim satisfaction in those last words sent a tingle of apprehension through Jessica. Gideon didn't know Rex. There was nothing that gave Rex more pleasure than coming out on top in a power-game. She had once admired and applauded his cleverness, but now she saw it as ruthless ego that had to be continually fed.

It was on the tip of her tongue to warn Gideon that he should take more care in his manner towards him, but then she reasoned that a man of Gideon's power was virtually untouchable. What could Rex do to him? Gideon, like Pillatoro, seemed inviolable.

She wished that she could reach him, touch him, but despite the moments of closeness tonight, he was still as distant from her as ever. Then, in a blindingly abrupt change of mood, he smiled at her, a warm smile that sent a tingle of pleasure through her whole body.

'Goodnight, Jessica,' he said softly. 'I hope the sun shines for you tomorrow.'

'Thank you,' she said on a buoyant note of happiness. 'Goodnight, Gideon,' she added more reluctantly, knowing she was dismissed, but loath to leave him.

But she took the memory of his smile away with her and hugged it with a fierce possessiveness as she lay in the darkness of Luisa's room. And not once did she think of Rex Anderson.

CHAPTER SEVEN

THE visitors from the Cultural and Heritage Commission had been and gone long before Sam and Jessica returned to Pillatoro the next evening. To Jessica's relief, Gideon made no comment on their visit during the conversation over the dinner-table. In fact his manner was less austere than usual. He even laughed over one of Sam's droll comments on amateur sailors.

'You should have invited Bernadette to go with you,' he remarked, which immediately dimmed Jessica's pleasure.

'What Jessica lacked in sailing expertise, she more than made up for in company,' Sam declared grandly, and gave her a particularly warm smile.

All day she had wondered if Sam was seriously attracted to her, as Gideon's questions had suggested last night, but there had been nothing but open friendliness in Sam's manner while they had been sailing. She hoped it would stay that way.

'Have you made much progress on the project, Jessica?' Gideon suddenly asked.

'I've been through all your father's work now,' she was happy to answer. 'I'll start checking his findings on Monday.'

The relaxed atmosphere came to an abrupt halt.

'What are you checking?' The sharp steel in Gideon's voice was enough to cut anyone dead.

Jessica's blood ran cold. She chose her words very carefully. 'A lot of your father's work is interpretative. He may have favoured one fact more than another, and looked for his proof from a mistaken point of view. In historical research, one must weigh every fact for its most likely perspective in the whole.'

'My father spent years sifting and weighing facts,' he reminded her with icy condescension.

'I know that,' she said quietly. 'But the proof eluded him. The reason may be that he placed too much importance on one fact and did not see the full significance of another. I would not be doing the job you employed me for if I didn't check everything.'

'Well, that sounds reasonable to me,' Sam put in heartily.

Gideon's hard gaze did not move from Jessica's. 'I think it's also reasonable that you give me a report on your progress. I will be home all day Friday. You can tell me then what plan of action you have in mind.'

'Very well,' she murmured, her heart sinking at the prospect of fighting Gideon's closed mind over the outcome of his father's theory.

It worried her very deeply. While she understood Gideon's need to have his father honoured as a man of vision, Jessica was already aware from Richard Cavilha's notes that he had taken a hobbyist's attitude to historical research, rather than a professional one. That did not make him wrong in his theory, but his reasoning was suspect.

More than suspect, Jessica was forced to acknowledge as she painstakingly checked the evi-

dence that Richard Cavilha had accepted on face
value. She went over detail after detail, desperately
seeking some assurance that she was wrong. Any
cross-data on the subject was so limited. It was difficult to actually pin anything down with absolute
certainty, but she knew that some of Richard Cavilha's conclusions were incorrect.

Yet Gideon would surely hate her if she dis-
credited his father's theory. He would probably
throw her out of Pillatoro. He would never accept
it...that this one most important purpose was even
being questioned, let alone professionally chal-
lenged. To him it would be another dream turning
to ashes.

She could not eat any breakfast on Friday
morning. Her stomach was a knot of sickening
tension. She swallowed down a cup of coffee, then
hurried off to the library. Doris arrived. Jessica gave
her some notes to type up. She knew that any more
checking was futile, but she went through the
mechanical process of appearing to work.

It was just after ten o'clock when Gideon opened
the library door. Jessica's heart stopped. Today, of
all days, he gave her a half-smile with his greeting,
and Jessica felt even more of a traitor to his cause.

'I'll be free for a while at one o'clock. I realise
that's your usual lunch-hour, but arrange with Mrs
Price to have it earlier,' he commanded in his autocratic way.

Then he was gone and relief surged through her.
She had a few more hours left. The time of reck-
oning would come. That was inevitable. But she
would never be ready for it.

'Shall I go and speak to Mrs Price now?' Doris asked in her efficient fashion.

Jessica hesitated, knowing it would be impossible to eat anything herself. Apart from this, she did not want Doris in the library while Gideon was there. 'I'd rather have my lunch later, Doris. I won't need you here while I give my report to Mr Gideon, so why don't you arrange to have yours in the kitchen at the usual time?'

Doris shrugged. 'Suits me. Sure you won't need me here for anything?'

'Positive,' Jessica asserted firmly, and was intensely grateful when Doris fell in with her wishes without argument.

The minutes ticked by, each one increasing Jessica's sense of doom. She could not bear the thought of leaving Pillatoro. Somehow she would have to make Gideon see... make him accept that this wasn't the way to honour his father. There had to be another answer, but when one o'clock came she hadn't found it.

Doris left the library.

Gideon entered.

The time had come, and the truth had to be told.

Gideon looked indomitable, a man who stood astride his world despite the personal tragedies which would have dragged any lesser person down. Yet Jessica knew he was vulnerable. He sank into one of the leather armchairs near her desk with a contented air. The midnight-blue eyes gleamed with eager interest, inviting her to tell him what he wanted to hear. What she had to say would kill that light, and everything within Jessica shrank from the darkness which would follow.

Without any presentiment of doom at all, he calmly lit the fuse of the bomb that Jessica had to explode. 'Now, tell me how far you've progressed and what plan of action you have in mind.'

Emotion fought logic, urging her to lie, to say anything but the truth which was such a leaden weight on her heart. 'Your...your father was a very brilliant man...'

The half-smile curved his lips and Jessica's hands began to tremble. She pressed them tightly together. Her throat was impossibly dry. She swallowed convulsively then forced out more words.

'For someone untrained in research, he's done a remarkable job of amassing facts to...to support his theory. But...' Fear paralysed her vocal chords.

Gideon frowned. 'But what?'

She could not lie. Every instinct told her that Gideon was too perceptive to let any sign of evasion slip by him anyway. Even now his eyes were sharply probing hers. 'But...he didn't give sufficient weight to the facts which did not support his theory.'

Gideon's face tightened. The fingers which had been spread over the ends of the armrests clenched into fists. 'What are you telling me?' he grated.

'It couldn't have been de Sequeira. Your father's theory is wrong in detail, if not in substance. He made the mistake of...' The words blurted out in a despairing rush.

Instantly he was on his feet. 'No!' The word exploded from him. He straightened up, his whole bearing one of untouchable dignity, his eyes burning with scorn. 'My father worked on this project for years. He poured his life into it after my mother died. You didn't even have a grounding in the subject a few weeks ago. How dare you set yourself up as a judge of his work?'

The blood drained from her face. 'I'm sorry,' she whispered shakily, 'but any good researcher will tell you the same thing.'

'You're not even good enough to follow in my father's footsteps!'

'No, I'm not,' she agreed sadly. 'I'm not denying he was a great man, Gideon, but any professional historian will shoot his theory down. It's full of holes.'

'He was right!' Gideon interrupted vehemently, and wheeled away from her, pacing the floor like a goaded lion. 'He has to be right! It can't be any other way! I won't have it any other way!' His eyes flashed a scathing indictment at her. 'I'll get someone else to prove it. You're the one who's incompetent.'

For a long moment Jessica stared at him in bleak resignation. She had known the axe must fall, and it had fallen on cue, but behind the fury of the man she saw the pain, and the pain would surely be repeated if she gave up now. 'It will make no difference, Gideon. You'll get the same result. There may have been some other Portuguese navigator who mapped the east coast of Australia, but it wasn't de Sequeira.'

Every stiff line of his body bristled with aggression. His eyes were narrowed slits of ice. 'How do you know that? I've been through my father's work, detail after detail, and it all fits.' He lifted a hand and clenched it, shaking it at her in challenge. 'You have no sense of vision. None at all! I should never have hired you for the job. It was plain from the start...' His hand opened in a gesture of dismissive disgust as he turned away. 'You're fired! Pack up and get out!'

The pain in her chest was so bad it took all Jessica's will-power to form the necessary words to counter-challenge him. 'Do you want someone who will just blindly follow your orders and fake what you want? What kind of monument would that be to your father, or your family,...to publish a theory which can and will be torn to pieces? Your father would be mocked, not revered for the wonderful man he was. Is that what you want to achieve?'

He was coming at her even as she spoke, his eyes shooting fire, his face working with a primitive savagery that threatened physical violence.

Instinct told Jessica to remain absolutely still. Despite her inner torment she met Gideon's blazing gaze with the calm serenity that comes when there is no other stand to be taken in a battle that has to be fought.

He stopped abruptly, his hands clenched tightly at his sides. 'What...do...you...know...of... my...father?' Each word was bitten out with venomous fury.

'Only what you and Sam have told me. And what his notes revealed of himself,' she answered quietly. 'But it's enough for me to respect him too deeply to aid you in damaging his reputation in any way. No matter what you feel, Gideon,' she added softly, compassion squeezing her heart.

His head jerked back as though she had hit him. A cold, cold pride settled over his features and if looks could kill, Jessica felt she would have been turned to stone at that very moment.

A knock on the library door startled both of them. Gideon turned as his personal secretary poked her head around the door, apprehension stamped on her face.

'What is it?' Gideon snapped.

'I'm sorry, sir. Please excuse me. Mr Koukadis is here to see you.' She was wringing her hands.

'Tell him to wait.' Each word was enunciated with slow and icy precision.

The secretary bolted without a backward glance.

Gideon swung back to Jessica, his face as hard as granite. 'This is your last chance, Miss Trelawney. Just give me one example of my father's failure to cross-check his facts.'

It was unfair, totally arbitrary, but the acid in his voice told Jessica she had no choice in the matter. Her mind whirled with wild urgency and fastened on one irrefutable example.

'The calculations to correct for the distortions in the Dieppe maps. I don't have the mathematical knowledge to calculate the effect of the loxo-dromes, erration, magnetic variation in the compass and the other effects which need to be included. It needs an engineer or a cartographer of the highest order.'

Sheer venom flared from Gideon's eyes. 'My father was an engineer by training. Of international reputation. Did you know that?'

He banged his fist down on the desk, emphatically punctuating his words. 'Don't you think he would have taken the most meticulous care? Checking, and re-checking those figures!' he

shouted at the top of his lungs, at the very limits
of exasperation. The totally controlled man was out
of control.

Doris opened the door.

'Get out!' he yelled, his hand slashing the air in
savage dismissal.

The door was hastily slammed.

Gideon's eyes stabbed Jessica with intense
bitterness.

'I'm sure he did,' Jessica answered shakily, 'but
it's essential for any kind of proof that those cor-
rections be independently confirmed.'

'That is for me to decide,' he thundered, and if
the walls had not been so solid they would surely
have been shaken by the violent volume of his voice.

'No,' Jessica said more firmly, aware that
everyone at Pillatoro had either heard or knew of
their argument now. Not that it mattered. Only the
issue at stake mattered. Gideon had to be stopped
from pursuing a futile and soul-destroying course
of action.

His face blazed with outraged authority. 'I make
the decisions here. I give the orders. And I will be
obeyed!'

A sense of utter defeat dragged through her heart.
Gideon would never yield, yet she had no choice
but to fight on. Jessica mustered the last of her
reserves. Her voice was almost a whisper as she
made her last-ditch stand.

'This is not your field of expertise, Gideon.
Whatever you say, your father's theory is wrong in
detail. If there is any hope for it, the only course
you can take is one of professional integrity. I believe that your father wouldn't want his work pub-

lished on any other basis, and you will only be doing him a terrible dishonour if you persist in doing what you want.'

He walked around the desk and came to a halt in front of her. Jessica looked up into eyes which would haunt her dreams for the rest of her days; eyes that were hard coals of darkness which stared through her as if she and everything else had ceased to exist. His face worked with uncontrollable emotion for several, long, agonising moments, then suddenly tightened into a grim mask.

'You've had your chance. I was a fool to...'

His mouth tightened over whatever words had been on his tongue. He turned away from her, his back stiff and unyielding. He moved to the door with all the rigid dignity of a pall-bearer. He opened the door and closed it quietly behind him, still without another word spoken or any recognition of Jessica at all. It was the end.

She was left in a silence so profound and disturbing that only the severe constriction in her chest forced her to breathe. She sat there too dazed to do anything else. Her heart beat painfully for Gideon. The project had meant so much to him. Too much. Her negation of his father's theory had ripped him apart.

Doris eventually crept back into the office. She opened her mouth, took one look at Jessica's white face, and closed it again. The violence of Gideon's outrage and fury had surely affected everyone in the building. Apprehension was in every one of Doris's movements as she went to her desk and very quietly got on with some work. Jessica did not attempt to do anything. She just sat, wrapped in a misery which had no cure.

It was exactly seven minutes past four when Jessica realised that she loved Gideon Cavilha. She had been staring blindly at the clock for some time. The terrible realisation made her notice it. And she knew exactly what that love meant . . . irrevocable, eternally binding, complete and without any mitigation . . . and the terrible part was, there was nothing, not one thing in the whole world that she could do for him or herself. He had fired her. He was sending her away. She had to leave Pillatoro. She would most probably never see him or Pillatoro again.

Jessica shook her head in despair, then on some blind impulse she stood up and walked over to the spiral staircase which led up to the observatory. She thought of Richard Cavilha building it after his wife had died, sitting up there and communing with the stars and the sea and the sky in his loneliness. It seemed appropriate that she should end her time here in the same place.

'Jessica . . .' Doris called softly.

She looked back at the secretary, saw the sympathetic concern on the older woman's face, and managed the wobbliest of tortured smiles. 'There's nothing you can do for me, Doris. Nothing anyone can do. It was . . .' Tears blurred her eyes and she choked out the last words. 'It was nice working with you.'

Then she hurried up the stairs to save the kindly secretary from making any reply. Words would have caused a flood of tears, and for some reason that

THE JOKER GOES WILD!

Play
this
card
right!

See
inside!

IT'S A WILD, WILD, WONDERFUL
FREE OFFER!

HERE'S WHAT YOU GET:

1. *Four New Harlequin Presents® Novels—FREE!* Everything comes up hearts and diamonds with four exciting romances — yours FREE from Harlequin Reader Service. Each of these brand-new novels brings you the passion and tenderness of today's greatest love stories.

2. *A Useful, Practical Digital Clock/Calendar—FREE!* As a free gift simply to thank you for accepting four free books we'll send you a stylish digital quartz clock/calendar — a handsome addition to any decor! The changeable, month-at-a-glance calendar pops out, and may be replaced with a favorite photograph.

3. *An Exciting Mystery Bonus—FREE!* You'll go wild over this surprise gift. It will win you compliments and score as a splendid addition to your home.

4. *Money-Saving Home Delivery!* Join Harlequin Reader Service and enjoy the convenience of previewing eight new books every month, delivered to your home. Each book is yours for $1.99—26 cents less per book than what you pay in stores. And there is no extra charge for postage and handling. Great savings and total convenience are the name of the game at Harlequin!

5. *Free Newsletter!* It makes you feel like a partner to the world's most popular authors...tells about their upcoming books...even gives you their recipes!

6. *More Mystery Gifts Throughout the Year!* No joke! Because home subscribers are our most valued readers, we'll be sending you additional free gifts from time to time—as a token of our appreciation!

GO WILD
WITH HARLEQUIN TODAY— JUST COMPLETE, DETACH AND MAIL YOUR FREE-OFFER CARD!

PLAY THIS CARD RIGHT!

YES! Please send me my four Harlequin Presents novels FREE along with my free Digital Clock/Calendar and free mystery gift as explained on the opposite page.

108 CIH CANT

PLACE
JOKER
STICKER
HERE

NAME _____
(PLEASE PRINT)

ADDRESS _____ APT. _____

CITY _____

STATE _____ ZIP CODE _____

Prices subject to change. Offer limited to one per household and not valid to current Presents subscribers.

HARLEQUIN READER SERVICE®
"NO RISK" GUARANTEE

- There's no obligation to buy — and the free books remain yours to keep.
- You pay the lowest price possible and receive books before they appear in stores.
- You may end your subscription anytime — just write and let us know.

IT'S NO JOKE!

MAIL THE POSTPAID CARD AND
GET FREE GIFTS AND $9.00 WORTH OF
HARLEQUIN NOVELS — *FREE!*

really didn't matter Jessica wanted to preserve the few shreds of dignity that were left to her.

The observatory was built on the highest roof of Pillatoro and it was like being on top of the world. The circular wall was all glass except for the thin steel poles that supported the roof. This was cob-webbed with steel shutters to accommodate the huge telescope set on a central dais.

Jessica sank on to one of the lounge chairs scattered around the floor. She looked out upon Gideon's world and could not hold the tears back any longer. She felt utterly overwhelmed by the despair of loving a man who probably despised her, definitely disapproved of her, and certainly hated her for discrediting his father's theory. She cried her heart out, and when finally there were no more tears left, her head ached from the agonised thoughts which still tortured her mind.

Her hands moved automatically to take out the hairpins, releasing the weight of the coil around her crown. Unfettered, the long tresses tumbled over her shoulders and down her back. Jessica raked her fingers over her scalp but the pain did not ease. She slumped further down into the chair and stared bleakly at the horizon.

Pillatoro: meaning to set, as in the sun and the moon and the stars. With almost unbearable sadness Jessica watched the sun lower in the western sky, and felt that her life was setting with it. She knew there would be no other man for her. Somehow in a few brief weeks, Gideon Cavilha had stamped himself upon her soul for ever.

The cloud formation was shot with red and gold, the colours gradually softening through pinks and oranges, slowly darkening and losing the brilliance of their hues. The violet tones gathered, deepening into the purples and greys of twilight. Then the sun was gone, as it had gone out of her own life.

The first stars appeared in the sky. The darkness of night brought out more and more stars. Jessica wondered vaguely if there would be a moon. She did not move. She felt too drained and there was no reason to move. No one would want to see her or talk to her. She was now an outcast. She had watched the sun set. Why not the stars and the moon as well? The last day...the last night...it was right to make a vigil of it...like a wake for the dream that had died, even before it had been born.

Jessica did not notice the lessening of darkness as floodlights were switched on around the grounds. She did not hear the calls of people searching for her. She was encased in a loneliness too deep for anything to penetrate. Her eyes only saw the stars. Her ears only heard the grief in her heart. Time had no meaning.

Even when the lights in the observatory were switched on, she automatically squeezed her eyelids shut, blocking out the hurtful dazzle. Her cold, stiff hands were suddenly engulfed by a warm pressure that demanded her attention.

'Jessica...Jessica...' Samson's deep voice throbbed with urgency. It beat into her ears, forcing an entry through the protective fog which cocooned her tortured mind. Questions formed. Samson? What did he want? Why couldn't he leave her alone?

'Jessica!'

Harsh insistence. He was squeezing her hands. Her eyelids felt too heavy to lift, but she tried. Sam's face swam in front of her. He muttered something under his breath and then he was looming over her. She instinctively cringed away from him as his arms pushed under her. She was too weak to resist his strength.

He lifted her as easily as he would a rag doll and she sagged limply against his huge chest. She tried to say no, tried to form her lips into the word, but her head was whirling with dizziness and Sam's arms were holding her tightly, and they felt warm and safe.

He carried her out of the observatory and down the spiral staircase without even a hesitation in his footing. Jessica vaguely remembered that he had carried Gideon for five kilometres. He was so strong there was not even an acceleration of his breathing. She did not know where he was taking her. Did not care. She lay with her head against his great heart and her mind emptied of all thought. The voices floated over her head and they seemed to come from a great distance.

'Where was she?' Gideon, harsh and guttural.

Sam answered without pausing in his step, his tone equally harsh. And accusing. 'Where Doris suggested. Up in the observatory.'

'Is she all right?'

'No. She's not bloody well all right, Gideon! What the hell do you expect? She's been working all hours for you and you heard Mrs Price. No meals today and hardly anything to eat yesterday or the day before. Not to mention the fact that you saw fit to punch her guts out because she had the courage to tell you the truth.'

'You don't have to ram it down my throat!' Gideon snapped. 'I'll call a doctor.'

'You're the goddamned doctor! You did the damage, Gideon, and by God you're going to fix it up.'

No answer from Gideon. Like an irresistible force Sam paced through the long halls of Pillatoro and it seemed only moments before he was leaning over her, laying her gently on soft pillows. He tucked bedclothes around her and brushed the long strands of hair from her face.

She opened her eyes and tried to focus them on his face. She wanted to tell Samson that nothing could be gained by trying to force Gideon to act against his will, but she couldn't find the energy to speak.

'It will be all right, Jessica,' Sam said with infinite gentleness. 'This would never have happened if I'd been here this afternoon. You must promise me you won't leave.'

Jessica knew he didn't understand. Her eyelids dropped wearily over the bleak emptiness of her eyes, closing him out. She hadn't seen the stars and the moon set. She wished Samson had let her stay in the observatory. He meant well. He just didn't understand.

'Jessica, give me your promise!' Sam commanded urgently.

Jessica couldn't. She had to leave. Gideon didn't want her here any more. But in one sense she would never leave. Gideon and Pillatoro would never leave her heart. 'Never leave,' she murmured, more as an echo of her thought than in answer to Sam.

'Justice will prevail,' he muttered and the mattress lifted as he stood up.

'You go too far, Sam.'

Jessica winced at the biting tone of Gideon's voice. She turned her face into the pillow away from it.

'Not yet far enough, Gideon, but by God I'll get there!' Sam retorted with quiet ferocity. 'Now we're going to get Mrs Price to see to Jessica's needs, then you and I are going to talk. And I mean talk!'

The click of the door closing told Jessica they had gone. She was glad. Their words had stirred the pain again and she didn't want to feel any more. It was over. It had never been. Except in the private recesses of her soul where it would now stay for ever locked.

She did not hear Mrs Price come in. The sleep of utter exhaustion had anaesthetised all her senses. The housekeeper gently loosened Jessica's clothes, took off her shoes and made sure she was warmly covered. She sat at the bedside for a long while and when finally she left the room it was with the certainty that Jessica's sleep was very heavy and would remain peaceful throughout the night.

CHAPTER EIGHT

CONSCIOUSNESS came slowly, weaving its way up through layers and layers of sluggish half-dreams that were vaguely disturbing. In an instinctive move to rid herself of them Jessica opened her eyes. It was an instant relief to see it was daylight, but the sight of Mrs Price sitting by her bed startled her.

'Ah, you're awake at last.' The housekeeper's face creased in kindly concern. 'And how are you feeling this morning?'

Jessica rubbed at her forehead, trying to clear the muzziness from her mind. The memories of yesterday came flooding back and she winced in pain.

'Is your head aching, dear? There's some Panadol in the bathroom.'

Mrs Price was instantly on her feet and Jessica put out a hand to stop her. 'No, I just...' She closed her eyes again, not wanting to face the day.

'Now you're not to worry about yesterday,' Mrs Price said hastily. 'Mr Samson said to assure you that everything's been sorted out and you're staying right here.'

Jessica's head whirled. How could it be sorted out? She vaguely remembered the anger in Sam's voice as he had spoken to Gideon last night. She couldn't recall the exact words he had said. Had Sam somehow forced Gideon to give her another chance?

'I'm sure you'll feel better when you've had a good, solid breakfast,' Mrs Price rattled on. 'This not eating has to stop.' She picked up the intercom and spoke to Annie, the cook, then addressed herself to Jessica again in a firm, motherly tone. 'I'm going to see that you have a good meal if I have to feed it to you myself.'

Jessica managed a weak smile. 'I'm all right, Mrs Price.'

'All right?' the housekeeper scoffed. 'You certainly are not all right and you're to stay in bed all day today and be properly looked after.'

'But...'

'No buts about it. You gave us all a dreadful fright last night. Such a commotion! I've never known Mr Gideon to lose his temper before. And then Mr Samson raising the roof when he came home and heard what had happened. When you weren't in your room he set the whole staff to searching for you, all through the grounds and down along the beach. I've never known such a day! And night! It would never have happened in Mr Richard's time, I can tell you.'

There would have been no reason for it to happen in Mr Richard's time, Jessica thought with sad irony. 'I'm sorry I caused so much trouble,' she muttered despondently.

'You didn't cause the trouble, dear, and don't you be thinking it,' Mrs Price chided kindly. 'You're a good, hard-working, honest girl, as I told Mr Gideon, myself. And he'll be along later on to talk to you. When you feel up to it.'

A convulsive shudder ran through Jessica. She couldn't face Gideon again. He hated her.

'Now you don't have to see him if you don't want to, dear. I'll tell Mr Samson ...'

'No. It's...it's all right, Mrs Price.' She couldn't imagine how it would be, but she didn't want to cause any more trouble between Samson and Gideon. She knew how deeply Gideon loved his brother and she did not want to compound the pain she had given him yesterday.

The housekeeper looked doubtful. 'Well, only if you're sure. I know Mr Gideon doesn't want to upset you again.'

Jessica was distressed by her own weakness when she slid out of bed to go to the bathroom. She felt giddy and faint, and but for Mrs Price's quick support she doubted that she would have stayed upright. The housekeeper fussed around, helping her wash and change into a nightie, then piling pillows up so that she would be comfortable to eat breakfast.

Jessica tried to do justice to the meal, but her appetite was non-existent and only her determination to feel stronger forced some of the food down. Mrs Price finally gave up urging her to eat more and departed with the tray. It was something of a relief to be left alone. Much as Jessica had appreciated Mrs Price's kindness, she had not been given any time to think since she had woken up, and she had a lot to think about.

Apparently Sam had accepted her point of view in regard to publishing his father's work and had argued the case with Gideon. 'Justice will prevail'...the words came back to her although she could not remember the context in which they had been spoken.

Justice was all very fine, but as far as Jessica could see, the case was hopeless anyway, because Gideon didn't want any other result but the one he had set her to prove. Since that result was now impossible, there was no longer any reason for him to keep her in his employ. Any meeting now could only be painful to both of them.

Tears welled up in Jessica's eyes and trickled down her cheeks. She brushed them away and swallowed the lump of emotion in her throat. She had done enough crying. Mrs Price had said that Gideon did not want her to be upset, so she wouldn't be upset, at least not on the surface.

The knock on her door set Jessica's heart thumping in panic. 'Wait!' she called out frantically, swinging her legs out of bed and snatching up the silk and lace négligé that Mrs Price had left on the chair for her.

She fought off a wave of dizziness as she thrust her arms into the loose sleeves, then stood up long enough to let the silk fall around her. She wanted to sit in the chair, but already she was churning at the thought of confronting Gideon and she was afraid of feeling faint in his presence. Somehow she had to remain composed. She quickly slipped back into bed and bolstered herself against the pillows that Mrs Price had piled up for her.

'Come...' Her voice was a shaky croak. She forced more volume into it. 'Come in!'

A self-conscious flush burnt into her cheeks as the door opened. Samson walked in, and the relief to her screaming nerves was enormous. She even smiled at the big man whose eyes swept over her in sharp concern.

'You're looking much better than I expected,' he said with an answering smile.

'I'm fine really, Sam.' Her smile turned down into a grimace. 'A bit shaky on my legs, which seems rather silly, but apart from that I'm fine.'

He nodded, but there was a considering frown on his brow and his eyes searched hers questioningly.

'I'm sorry for collapsing on you last night. I didn't mean to worry you,' Jessica added in a guilty rush.

'It was my privilege to be able to help such a woman as you, Jessica,' he said with a deep, sonorous ring in his voice.

It embarrassed her. Although she had been aware that Sam admired her, the tone of his voice and the way he was looking at her now set Jessica's nerves on edge again. 'I...I wasn't being very sensible,' she muttered.

'Under the circumstances, I think you were remarkably strong and courageous,' Sam replied in complete seriousness.

It suddenly struck Jessica that she had never seen Sam so serious. His natural manner was one of bright cheerfulness, and although she had seen great sadness in him, this present demeanour reminded her too closely of Gideon, bringing home the fact that they were indeed brothers, in more than name.

He paced across the room with the air of a general in command; strong, forceful, authoritative. He paused by the drawn curtains, gazing out to sea for several long moments before turning back to her, determined purpose carved on every line of his face.

'Jessica, you feel Pillatoro, don't you?'

The question jolted her. She knew instantly what he meant, but she had thought that her empathy with this extraordinary place was something unique to herself, something bound up with her feeling for Gideon.

Sam did not wait for her answer. His blue eyes were flashing with absolute certainty as he walked towards her. 'It has to be so. I saw it seeping into you even on that first night. My mother told me how it affected her when she first came here, and I think it was the same for you. It lives for you, doesn't it, Jessica? Just as it does for me and Gideon. And that's why you fought him yesterday.'

He sat on the edge of her bed and picked up one of her hands, fondling it gently as he spoke on, his eyes never leaving hers. 'You care about Pillatoro. You care about what harm Gideon might do in his blind grief. You care about our father's reputation. And I think... I hope... you care about me, too,' he finished softly.

His eyes looked for an affirmation and Jessica could not deny the truth of his perception. A sense of hopelessness dragged her voice to a whisper as she gave her reply. 'Yes, I care, Sam. I've been here such a little time, but...' She gave an ironic shrug. 'I'll always remember it.'

'Jessica, you mustn't leave.'

She shook her head sadly. 'I can't stay now, Sam. There's no reason for...'

'Yes, there is.' His eyes glittered with some intensely felt emotion. 'Forget the damned project! I want you to stay. For ever. I want you to marry me, Jessica.'

Shock rolled across her mind. Her heart squeezed into a tight ball. Sam meant it. Not for a moment could Jessica doubt that he had proposed marriage to her in all seriousness. The urgency in his eyes, the whole purposefulness of his manner proclaimed the fact.

He was squeezing her hand, revealing the agitation of his feeling, but Jessica felt completely confused. Sam had never given any indication of the depth of his feelings before. What a mess, she thought distractedly. What a horrible, hurtful mess!

And Sam was such a great man! It seemed a terrible insult to refuse him, and yet refuse him she must. A great well of sadness filled her soul. She did not want to leave Pillatoro, and she would have done anything to avoid hurting Sam, but she could not love him as she loved his brother, and to marry him would be terribly, terribly wrong. Her eyes pleaded for his understanding as she carefully worded her reply.

'That is the greatest compliment I've ever been paid, Sam. Probably greater than I will ever be paid in my whole life. But I'm not worthy of it. You're a wonderful person and I do care for you, but not in the way that you'd want from your wife. I want the best for you, and I can't give you that. I'm sorry, but you must see I can't accept.'

He frowned, his gaze dropping from hers for a minute or two before lifting again in a cautious appeal. 'Jessica, I know this proposal is precipitate. We haven't known each other long. I spoke now because I want you to stay here and I have to leave tomorrow on a tour of charity concerts which were booked some time ago. But I can cancel my performances! I'll give them the money. This is more important to me. If we spent the time together...'

'No,' she interrupted gently but firmly. The pain of her own unrequited love filmed her eyes with tears. 'I'm sorry, Sam. I truly am deeply sorry, but there's no chance I'll change my mind. I...I love someone else, you see. It's quite futile, and it'll never come to anything, but I can't stop loving him.'

To her intense embarrassment she saw compassion in his eyes. 'Gideon told me that you had recently lost someone you loved. That was why I refrained from pressing you with...with what I wanted. I thought perhaps in time...'

'No.' Her cheeks burnt with shame over the misconception, but she saw no point in correcting it. It would probably hurt Sam more if she told him it was his brother she loved. 'I know that all the time in the world won't make any difference to how I feel about him,' she said unequivocally.

Sam heaved a sigh and shook his head. 'You're so like one of us, Jessica.' He stroked her hand for several long, silent minutes before adding, 'I still want you to stay at Pillatoro. You mustn't leave, Jessica. Promise me you'll be here when I come back.'

'Sam...' More tears gathered and she had to swallow hard to keep in check the sobs that threatened to erupt. 'I can't stay if Gideon doesn't want me here. You must know that.'

His face set in grim determination. 'Gideon will ask you to stay.'

'That's not the same thing, Sam.' She turned her head away, unable to fight the tears any longer.

He gently squeezed her hand. 'Jessica, I know how rough Gideon was on you yesterday, but I assure you that's over. He knows he was wrong. He will respect your opinion. My brother is essentially a fair man. A kind man. Don't judge him on yesterday, Jessica. Give him another chance. Will you do that?'

She nodded, too choked to argue.

Sam stood up, leaned over, and pressed a soft kiss on her temple. 'Stay, Jessica. I don't know how or why, but Pillatoro needs you. I feel it very strongly. I won't bother you with this matter again, but you must stay.' He stood there, gently stroking her hair, and his voice was a low murmur that was like a further caress. 'We could have made a great team. Taken on the whole world. It's a damned shame.'

He heaved a sigh and left her side, walking slowly to the door. He paused for a moment, then looked back at her with all the dignity of a great man. 'If there is anything you want, Jessica, at any time, you know you can always come to me and I'll be there waiting for you.' Then with a brief nod, and without pausing for any reply from her, he opened the door and left.

His parting words had not been a mere gesture. Jessica knew Sam was not the type of person who made empty gestures. He was totally sincere. But did he really love her or had he been influenced by her feeling for Pillatoro? He had not declared love, and she hoped with all her heart that he did not feel as bereft as she did herself.

Sam's proposal preyed on her mind for the rest of the morning. Mrs Price brought her a luncheon tray and clucked in concern when Jessica could not eat as much as the housekeeper considered beneficial. However, the kindly woman refrained from nagging and urged Jessica to have a good long afternoon nap. Emotionally drained from the scene with Sam and her worry over another confrontation with Gideon, Jessica did sleep.

It was late afternoon when she awoke, and when she got up to go to the bathroom she was relieved to find that the giddy weakness had diminished considerably. She slapped cold water over her face and brushed her hair, and felt even better. Reluctant to return to bed, she opened the door on to the balcony and stood there, enjoying the fresh breeze off the sea.

She moved out to the balustrade and was remembering her first night at Pillatoro and Gideon's kiss when the knock came on her bedroom door. She jerked around, her heart suddenly in her mouth. For the life of her she could not speak, and she watched in fearful fascination as the door opened and Gideon stepped into the room.

Surprise flitted over his face when he saw the empty bed. His gaze swept around and found her. He walked swiftly through the room, then hesitated at the door, tension in every line of his body. He looked so austere, so formidable, that fear kept Jessica silent. When he spoke, the effort to do so was obvious.

'I'm sorry. I thought you might still be asleep so I...' He paused, made an impatient gesture. 'I wanted to check that you were...not in need of anything.'

It was a strangely awkward speech from Gideon. His ill-ease had the perverse effect of unfreezing Jessica's tongue. 'I'm fine now...thank you,' she said stiffly.

'I'm...relieved to hear it. Is there anything you'd like...some afternoon tea...?'

'No, thank you. Mrs Price has been looking after me very well.'

They stared at each other across the balcony, the memory of yesterday's traumatic meeting pulsing between them, filling the silence with almost unbearable tension. Gideon's face looked tightly drawn and the shadows around his eyes suggested that he had not slept at all. When he finally spoke again, his voice held a brittle note of strain.

'I've spent considerable time wrestling with my conscience, and I must acknowledge how wrong I was yesterday. I appreciate how very difficult I made it for you to tell me the truth. I reacted very badly. I want to apologise for what I said to you, and the manner in which I said it. Both were uncalled for, and totally undeserved. I have no excuse to offer. I can only say how very deeply I regret everything that happened, and hope you can find it in your heart to accept my apology.'

Jessica knew how much that speech must have cost him. Gideon Cavilha had probably never apologised for anything before in his whole life. Humility did not come naturally to him.

Her gaze dropped to the envelope which he was holding, and even while her mind registered the effort Gideon had made on her behalf, she was sickened by the thought of what was in that envelope. No doubt it would contain a handsome

cheque. No one could call Gideon Cavilha mean.
She lifted bleak eyes to his and some of her inner
desolation crept into her voice.

'I didn't want to hurt you. You'll never know
how much it cost me... to tell you the truth.' She
dragged in a deep breath. 'There's no need for you
to apologise. As long as you now believe what I
said, none of the rest really matters.'

He frowned, and his face suddenly broke into a
pained grimace. It startled Jessica to see the iron
control which Gideon had always projected slipping
away in front of her. The tension became palpable.
The dark eyes stabbed across at her in probing
concern. 'You were right in everything you said,
Jessica. I don't dispute that any more. But I can't
dismiss the rest so easily.'

The rest... what was the rest to him? His loss of
control? Certainly not love. It would never be love,
Jessica thought despairingly. 'Please... I'd rather
not talk about it. It's... it's over. I'd be grateful if
you'd just let it be.'

He shook his head as if he didn't want to accept
her answer, then reluctantly muttered, 'As you
wish.' His gaze dropped to the envelope he held,
and his fingers rubbed over it several times before
he stepped out on to the balcony and handed it to
her. 'This letter came for you in the afternoon post
yesterday. I'm afraid it was overlooked until today.
I hope it's not anything urgent.'

Jessica's hand trembled from the sheer force of
her relief as she took it. A letter, not a cheque from
Gideon. She could not have borne it if he had
started to talk severance pay to her.

'Perhaps you should read it,' Gideon suggested as she stared blindly at the envelope.

Her fingers mechanically tore it open and extracted the letter. She obeyed Gideon's suggestion without thinking, grateful for some distraction from his disturbing closeness. It was some moments before she realised that the letter was from Rex. The contents struck her with savage irony. He was virtually guaranteeing her a lectureship at Sydney University, and he wanted her to come back. Dawn had been a mistake.

Another mistake! A hysterical little laugh bubbled out of Jessica's throat. Then she looked up into Gideon's eyes and the laugh abruptly died. Oh God! She loved him so desperately! She quickly dropped her gaze to the letter again, folding it meticulously as she tried to contain the pain in her heart.

'Why did you laugh like that, Jessica?' Gideon demanded tautly.

A tide of hot blood scorched into her cheeks. 'I've . . . I've just been offered another job.'

'From Anderson?'

The question startled her into meeting his gaze and the dark turbulence in his eyes startled her further. 'Yes. He . . . he wants me to go back to the university. There's a lectureship coming up.'

Gideon's hands suddenly lifted and grasped her upper arms. 'Is there no hope then?'

The urgently spoken query seemed to leave so much unsaid. But the look in his eyes . . . Jessica's heart suddenly accelerated to a thunderous tempo. He cared about her. He wanted her to stay. He really did. She hastily worked some moisture into her dry mouth. 'If you want me to investigate further, I think much of your father's work can...'

'You'll go on?'

'Yes,' she whispered hopefully.

'Thank God!' he sighed, but still there was that dark turbulence in his eyes, and his fingers pressed into the soft flesh of her arms. 'Anderson's not good enough for you, Jessica. The man is worthless. Don't ever go back to him. I'll pay you whatever a lectureship is worth. More. Anything you like. You can do the research on your own terms. I promise you I won't interfere.'

She barely heard the offer. His first words writhed through her mind, stirring horror and humiliation.

'You knew?' she whispered, absolutely stricken that nothing had been hidden from him that first day. And he thought she loved Rex...still loved him!

He muttered something under his breath, and clearly in some torment of mind, he swept her into a tight embrace. 'Don't look like that!' he murmured hoarsely, moving his lips over her hair with a passion that had nothing to do with giving comfort.

Jessica's emotions were in such turmoil she couldn't think at all. Gideon was holding her, just as she wanted him to, but somehow it was because of Rex, which was not at all what she wanted. And Gideon knew about Rex.

'He's not worthy of your love, Jessica. He sold you out, didn't he?' Gideon stated with hissing contempt.

'Yes,' she admitted helplessly. 'But I don't love him. I didn't. He...' Impossible to explain. 'It was all a mistake,' she finished limply.

Gideon's chest heaved as he sucked in a long breath, and she felt the warm whisper of it through her hair. 'Then you'll stay here at Pillatoro?'

I'll stay here for ever if you want me to, Gideon, Jessica thought dizzily. Her body was reacting to his, tingling with awareness, wanting to press closer.

'Jessica...answer me!'

His fingers threaded through her hair, tugging her head back, forcing her to meet his eyes. She could not hide her agony of heart and mind, and she was afraid how much he would see. Her lips quivered as she answered, 'If you want me to.'

A pained look crossed his face and he shook his head. Jessica started to tremble from the terrible force of her emotion as he loosened his embrace, his hands moving to her shoulders, his body drawing away.

'No, I have no right to force my will on you, Jessica. God knows I tried yesterday, and I won't do it again.' Nevertheless, the midnight-blue eyes carried an urgent appeal. 'I do want you to stay, on any terms you'd like to make, but it must be what you want too.'

The relief was earthshaking. It thundered through Jessica like a tidal wave, washing away the torment of the last twenty-four hours. Gideon did not hate her. He wanted her to stay. He actually cared so much about it that he was prepared to do anything to meet her needs. He was not just being kind or fair. He *wanted* her to stay!

On top of the relief came a host of questions that had been gnawing at her mind for weeks. Why had

Gideon given her the job? What were his feelings towards her? Surely this was the time to ask. She took a deep breath and screwed up her courage. Even in this conciliatory mood, Gideon was not a man to challenge lightly.

'There are some things I want to know, Gideon.'

Jessica was unaware of the stubborn tilt of her chin, the quiet glint of determination in her eyes, the firm steadiness of her voice; but some of Gideon's tension eased as she exhibited the signs of the inner strength he had come to recognise.

'Tell me,' he invited quietly.

'If you were aware...' Jessica had to force herself to go on, '...what Rex was doing to me that day, why did you hire me?'

A reminiscent smile softened Gideon's mouth as he gently stroked Jessica's hair back from her shoulders. She stood absolutely still, revelling in the light brush of his fingers. 'You reminded me of Luisa,' he murmured, then lifted eyes which held a tenderness that was more than compassion. 'That day in Anderson's office. You looked so bereft, so hopeless... it tugged at my heart. The urge to play the part of Saint Jude became irresistible.'

'I'm glad you did,' Jessica whispered huskily.

The faint smile turned into a grimace. 'Even after yesterday?'

'Yes.'

He sighed. Very slowly the faint smile crept back, and for the first time Jessica saw admiration in his eyes. 'You are like Luisa, Jessica. You have the same quality of strength that will endure, even under the greatest of adversities.'

She reached out and touched him, her palm lightly resting on his chest, instinctively placed over his heart. 'It's you who have the strength, Gideon,' she said softly, and her own heart beat faster as she added, 'Sam told me about your family, how they died with your father. I'm sorry I couldn't do what you wanted for him. I know how much it meant to you.'

She only saw a glimmer of the pain before he shut his eyes. His whole body tensed, then he shook his head and his hand came up to cover hers, squeezing it tightly as he met her anxious gaze. 'I was wrong, Jessica. You were right. And I want you to keep working on the substance of the theory. If it can't be proved... well, at least we pursued my father's work. I think he would have liked that, don't you?'

She smiled in relief. 'Yes. He would want the truth. It can't be de Sequeira, but it's possible it may have been someone else. Perhaps Mendonca. What we need to do...'

She faltered. Gideon was smiling at her. Really smiling. And her heart was jumping all over the place.

'I'm glad you don't love Anderson, Jessica. And I'm glad you're staying on,' he said with rich satisfaction in his voice. His hand lifted hers away from him but he held it securely. 'I don't want to tire you out, but I would like to hear all that you could have told me yesterday, if I'd been willing to listen.'

He drew her back over to the bed and urged her to lie down again while he settled himself on the chair beside her. The hours that followed were absolutely blissful to Jessica. Gideon showed an avid interest in everything she had to say, and because he was so well informed on the subject himself, a quick understanding grew between them.

Gideon ordered that his dinner be brought with hers and Jessica found she had no trouble at all in enjoying the delicious meal that Mrs Price had organised. She exulted in the amazing change in Gideon's manner. He was so relaxed, so approachable; and after dinner he stayed on, obviously keen to continue their conversation.

'I must go and let you sleep,' Gideon said finally, offering her a rueful little smile. 'I've been talking too long. You shouldn't be such a good listener, Jessica.'

'I've enjoyed every minute of it,' she protested.

He stood up and picked up her hand, fondling it gently for several moments before he looked at her with an expression of soft contentment. 'I've enjoyed it too. Very much. Perhaps I was wrong about playing Saint Jude for you. I think he may have been there that afternoon, looking after me.' He leaned over and brushed his lips across her forehead. 'Goodnight, Jessica.'

He was at the door before she found breath enough to whisper, 'Goodnight, Gideon.'

He left her with a smile that tingled through her heart for a long time, filling it with pleasure and hope. Saint Jude...'the hope of the hopeless'...was he looking down on her and Gideon, tonight? she wondered whimsically.

It was enormously pleasing to think she had somehow given new hope to Gideon. Hope for what, she wasn't sure, but she could rest secure with the happy thought that Gideon did feel something for her, something very positive. And that thought put a smile on her lips as she drifted into sleep.

CHAPTER NINE

JESSICA was perfectly well the next morning. Her happiness over the change in Gideon's manner towards her was only dimmed by the memory of the pain she had given Sam. She could not help thinking that his departure today was fortunate timing, yet she hated the thought of his being miserable over her while he was away. But there was nothing she could do. What he wanted of her was not in her power to give.

Gideon had told her he would be flying Sam to Mascot Airport after lunch. Jessica knew that both brothers would expect her in the dining-room for that farewell meal, but she was extremely conscious of the fact that she would be sitting between the man whose love she wanted, and the man whose love she had just rejected. As it turned out, Jessica found the situation even more difficult than she had anticipated. Bernadette Adriani was also there.

Jessica's heart plummeted when she saw the beautiful girl. The momentous happenings over the last two days had driven Bernadette from Jessica's mind, but one look at the girl brought back the misery of knowing where Gideon's true affections lay. Although his manner no longer held that austere reserve towards Jessica, she did not feel consoled by it.

Sam, however, was a pillar of strength. Not by word or manner did the big man even hint at what had passed between them yesterday. He had declared he would not bother Jessica with any further declaration, and true to his word, the attention he gave her was every bit as brotherly as that he gave Bernadette. Nevertheless, Jessica was very conscious of a depth of feeling in his satisfaction that she was indeed staying on at Pillatoro.

When the planned time of departure came, Jessica and Bernadette accompanied the two men out to the front courtyard to wave them off. As they walked through the great hall Jessica took secret pleasure in the dappled light from the stained-glass window, until the thought came to her that Saint Jude could do nothing to help Sam if he truly loved her. She hoped that it was not so, that he would find the happiness he deserved with another woman.

'Stay here,' Gideon commanded, halting them under the great arch which framed the entrance doors. 'Once the helicopter blades start up you'll get blown away if you come down to the courtyard.'

Sam enveloped Bernadette in a brief bear-hug, kissed the curls on the top of her head, then grinned down at her. 'I'll have to be telling your father to load his shotgun. You've grown up so very beautiful,' he said indulgently.

Then he turned to Jessica, the grin fading into a wan smile as he took her hands in his. The twinkle in his eyes dimmed, swallowed up by a tenderness that squeezed Jessica's heart.

'Be happy here,' he said softly. He let her go, started to turn away, hesitated, then swung back to her, a poignant longing in his eyes. 'Jessica . . .'

The choked emotion in the way he said her name created instant tension. Jessica was intensely aware of Gideon's and Bernadette's utter stillness, and her own embarrassment at Sam's revelation of feeling was swamped by a deep compassion for the pain he had so valiantly hidden up until this moment.

Even now he was struggling to hold back, speaking in short bursts. 'The concert in Melbourne...it's to be telecast nationally. I'll be singing Mahler's "Songs of a Wayfarer". If you have the chance, listen to it. I'm dedicating the last song to you, the one that commences, "*Die zwei blauen Augen von meinem Schatz*".'

He paused, took a deep breath, and a sad resignation clouded his eyes as he softly translated.

' "My sweetheart's blue eyes
have driven me into the world.
I must leave the place I love most.
Blue eyes, why did you look at me?
Now I must ever feel anguish and grief." '

'I think,' he added, almost in a whisper, 'I shall sing that rather well.'

Then he turned and strode down the steps, unaware of the pall of silence he left behind him.

Jessica instantly threw a plea for understanding at Gideon, but his face had the look of a frozen mask, the midnight-blue eyes darkened by an inner turbulence she could not read. He stepped stiffly to Bernadette who looked equally frozen. His arm curved around the young girl's shoulders, squeezing hard, as if to force warm life back into her veins. His gaze fastened on Jessica over Bernadette's head, and there was now a compelling plea in his eyes.

'Look after her. I must go.'

Then he was striding after Sam. Jessica looked uncomprehendingly at Bernadette. The girl was white-faced, trembling, but she held herself with upright dignity until the helicopter had lifted Sam out of sight. Only then did understanding dawn on Jessica. It was not Gideon who drew Bernadette to Pillatoro. It was Sam. And Gideon knew it.

She slid a sympathetic arm around Bernadette's waist, realising how deeply painful Sam's parting words must have been. 'Come inside, Bernadette,' she invited softly. 'I think we need to talk, you and I.'

'No...no, I...I have to go,' Bernadette choked out, resisting the tug of Jessica's hand.

'Bernadette, I don't love Sam. And I never will,' Jessica confided gently.

Tear-filled hazel eyes lifted their pain to the blue eyes that had captured Sam's heart. 'Oh, Jessica! He'll never love me now.'

The cry of despair rent Jessica's heart, for she knew all too well what Bernadette was feeling. She put her arms around the slight body which had begun to shudder with impending sobs. 'Come and sit down. We'll talk about it. Don't give up hope, Bernadette,' she soothed quietly, steering her back into the great hall, then into the library which was the closest room to hand.

Bernadette sank on to one of the armchairs and covered her face with her hands. 'I'll be all right in a minute,' she choked out. 'I'm sorry I...'

'I'm sorry too, Bernadette. I didn't know. I thought you and Gideon...' Jessica stopped, ashamed of the relief that was surging through her.

Bernadette shook her head. 'It's always been Sam. But he never sees me as anything but a little sister. Everyone else can see what I feel for him. But not Sam. Not Sam,' she sobbed despairingly.

Jessica remained silent, aware that there was nothing she could say to alleviate Bernadette's pain.

'I've loved Sam ever since I was a kid. Our families have always been close. He took me sailing with him just about as soon as I could walk. Gideon says ... but it won't happen now. I knew it that last weekend I was here. The way Sam looked at you ... talked about you ...' She lifted tear-washed eyes. 'I'm not blaming you, Jessica.'

'I know,' she murmured sympathetically.

'I came today because I still had to see him. It's stupid, I know. But I can't help it.'

'I don't think it's stupid,' Jessica assured her. 'Maybe one day Sam will see you as you want him to.'

Bernadette nodded sadly. 'Gideon says that.' She drew in a deep breath and offered a wobbly smile that was full of irony. 'I'm glad you don't love Sam, Jessica.'

It was on the tip of Jessica's tongue to say she was glad that Bernadette didn't love Gideon, but she clamped down on the words. They wouldn't help Bernadette and she didn't want to talk about what she felt for Gideon. 'Sam didn't think much of me as a sailor,' she offered as some measure of hope. 'Give it more time, Bernadette. Sam is a great man.'

'Yes. He is, isn't he?' The words carried a wealth of love. 'There's no one else like him.' She sighed and stood up. 'Thanks for being kind to me, Jessica. I'd better get on my way.'

'I'm sure Gideon would want you to stay,' Jessica said quickly.

Bernadette shook her head. 'No. Gideon will understand. Sam's gone.'

And that said it all.

Having seen Bernadette off, Jessica paused in the great hall and lifted her gaze to the picture of Saint Jude. She sent up a silent prayer for all of them...for Sam and Bernadette...Gideon and herself...wishing that that was how it could be.

With a heavy sigh she returned to the library, nursing one warming memory from Sam's traumatic farewell...Gideon's appeal to her to look after Bernadette. He had trusted her to comfort the girl...as he would have done...as he had done that afternoon in the library after Sam had returned from sailing with Bernadette and then come in search of Jessica. Jessica understood that embrace now. It was the same as Gideon had given her in Rex's office, imparting comfort and strength to a woman who had lost someone she loved. Unfortunately for Bernadette, her love for Sam was not a self-deluding infatuation, as Jessica's had been for Rex.

The thought reminded her of Rex's letter, which had to be answered. She sat down at her desk, intent on getting the distasteful task over and done with. It took several drafts before she was satisfied that her refusal of Rex's propositions was worded both tactfully and firmly. He did not deserve tact, but Jessica was now too wary of Rex's character to invite more vindictiveness from him. She knew that the lectureship was a bribe with strings attached, but it was still a large concession from him, and Rex was not going to take kindly to her rejection.

Having completed the letter and sealed it ready for the post, Jessica once more opened the fire-proof safe where Richard Cavilha's work was stored. Her gaze fell on the diary which was also stored there—Luisa's diary. Since Gideon had likened her to Luisa, Jessica was more curious than ever to read it, but it was written in Portuguese.

She had been tempted to ask Gideon to get it translated, but had shied away from doing so. It was a personal family memento and had nothing to do with the project on which she was engaged. Nevertheless, it intrigued her, as everything to do with Pillatoro had from the moment she had come here. Even more so now. She couldn't resist flicking through the pages, idly looking at the dates and names written in a small, neat hand.

The noise of the helicopter heralded Gideon's return. Jessica automatically listened to it land, listened for the opening of the front door, the foot-steps down the hall. She held her breath as they paused outside the library door, and then the door opened, and Gideon came in, his dark gaze sweeping straight to her as if he had known she would be there at her desk.

He closed the door and walked over to her, his gaze falling to the book in her hands. 'Luisa's diary?' he observed.

'Yes. I wish I could read it,' Jessica said wistfully.

'I'll get it translated for you.'

Just like that, Jessica thought, although she immediately told herself she shouldn't be surprised.

Gideon had been nothing if not generous to her. She watched him drop into the armchair near her desk, noting that his face held that tired, drawn look again.

'Thank you,' she murmured.

He waved a dismissive hand. 'Was Bernadette all right when she left?'

'She was calm. Resigned, I think.'

He nodded and sat in brooding silence for several minutes, but for once Jessica felt she was not shut out of his mind. They were sharing the memory of Bernadette's pain. And Sam's.

'Sam does love her, in his own way,' Gideon said with a sad shake of his head.

'But not in the way Bernadette wants,' Jessica added softly.

Gideon sighed and lifted his gaze to hers. 'There's nothing we can do.'

Jessica's heart leapt as he coupled her with himself, obviously taking it for granted that she understood all he implied. It was a tremendous relief to know he now accepted her assertion that she could never return Sam's love. 'Maybe time will sort it all out,' she murmured. 'We can only hope so.'

A half-smile softened his face. 'St Jude to the rescue again.'

Jessica smiled back. 'He's done very well so far.'

'Yes,' Gideon agreed quietly, and his eyes held a warmth for her that Jessica had never seen before. 'I've told you so much about my family, Jessica. I'd like to hear about yours. I want to know why you're alone. Why you had nowhere to go.'

Jessica squirmed between a need to share her life with him, and a reluctance to reveal a background which was so starkly different from his. Here at Pillatoro the social gap between them had become blurred, but once she spoke of her past, would it re-shape Gideon's opinion of her, make her less attractive to him?

'If it pains you to speak of it...'

He was frowning, and Jessica panicked at the swift shuttering of the warmth he had shown her. 'No! It's not painful.' She gave a rueful smile. 'Just a bit miserable, I guess.'

'Would you rather keep it to yourself?' he asked, and Jessica sensed he was teetering on the edge of withdrawal.

'No.' She determinedly pushed her doubts and fears aside. Retaining Gideon's interest was all that mattered. 'My family live at Broken Hill. My father and two brothers are miners, and my sister is married to another miner. I suppose you could say I was the cuckoo in the nest, because I wasn't interested in the kind of life my family led. And they didn't understand or approve of what I wanted to do.'

She drew in a quick breath. 'There were a lot of arguments over my staying on at school to get the Higher School Certificate, and when I wanted to go on to university... well, my father made it clear that if I wasn't prepared to settle down where I belonged, then he would wipe his hands of me and I could fend for myself.'

Jessica was unaware of the grim defiance that tightened her face as she continued her story. 'So I did just that. With the money I'd saved from baby-sitting jobs, I took the train to Sydney and got myself a job as a part-time waitress. I enrolled at the university and divided my time between work and study.'

'No social life?' Gideon asked softly.

Jessica shrugged. 'That first year my main motivation was to show my family I could do it. I couldn't afford distractions. I passed the examinations with high distinctions and I went home for Christmas, hoping to...'

She sighed and shook her head. 'It didn't mean anything to them. More than ever I was the cuckoo in the nest. I knew then that I would never belong there, and if I ever failed, there would be no sympathy for me at home.'

'That must have made you feel very alone,' Gideon commented sympathetically.

Jessica darted a quick glance at him and her heart turned over. The deep caring in the intense blue eyes was for her. And he understood the loneliness and the despair she had felt. There was not the slightest trace of critical judgement in his expression.

She took another deep breath and plunged on. 'I was doing majors in history, and in my third year at university, Professor Anderson took a number of his top students for special tutorials. He began to take a personal interest in me and I... for the first time in my life, I felt... valued by someone.'

She paused, groping for the right words to explain how deeply Rex's interest had affected her. 'Just the fact that he wanted to be with me gave me a sense of worth that I'd never had. And when he said he loved me...' She threw Gideon an anxious look of appeal. 'I thought he was everything I'd ever wanted.'

Gideon nodded encouragingly.

'And I hung on to that belief, right up until the day he told me it was over. The afternoon you came to the office... I felt I was nothing again. I don't know what I would have done if you hadn't rescued me,' she finished limply.

He smiled, a slow smile that showered her with approval and admiration. 'You would have picked yourself up and forged a new future for yourself, just as you did after your family had rejected you. Nothing will ever beat you, Jessica.'

Except my love for you, she thought, fiercely wishing she could reveal that truth. She forced a smile. 'Have I told you all you wanted to know?'

'Not all. But enough.' He stood up and took her hand, pressing it in emphasis as he spoke. 'Few people have the strength to act on their convictions, as you have done. You're worth a great deal, Jessica. Don't ever doubt that.'

His mouth curved in soft irony. 'As for Anderson, you were a victim of your own lack of self-confidence, Jessica. Don't reproach yourself for that. Any man who doesn't value what you are has to be a blind fool.'

He stopped, and every nerve in Jessica's body tingled with vibrant hope. The flash of intense need in his eyes, the sudden tension in the hand holding hers; then, even as excitement quivered through her, she saw his retreat: the quick inhalation of breath, the forced relaxation of muscles.

'It must be time for dinner,' he murmured.

Jessica felt dreadfully deflated. 'Yes. I suppose it is.'

He smiled. 'I'm glad we're alone and I don't have to share it with anyone else.'

Disappointment was instantly replaced by a zing of elation. 'I'm glad too.'

Gideon drew her out of her chair and they walked together, hand in hand, through the halls of Pillatoro, and that strong hand enfolding hers pumped a wild joy through Jessica's veins, and suddenly all the years that had led up to this moment were nothing. Nothing at all. Gideon wanted her with him, and her life was beginning now.

On Monday morning Jessica received several looks of surprise from the clerical staff, and most surprised of all was Doris. Her astonishment was instantly followed by a warm delight that everything had been smoothed over and the project was to be pursued. Time and again throughout the day Jessica caught the older woman looking at her with a kind of wondering awe, and finally she asked Doris the reason for it.

'I just can't get over it... Mr Gideon browbeating you the way he did and here you are, calmly forging ahead as though nothing had happened.' She shook her head in amazement.

Jessica smiled. 'Well, he's given me a free hand now. I couldn't ask for better conditions than that, could I?'

Doris rolled her eyes. 'Miracles will never cease,' she muttered and went on with her typing.

Jessica hoped Doris was right. She wanted two miracles: firstly that Gideon would come to love her as she loved him, and secondly that Sam would eventually love Bernadette. There was definitely some hope for the first, she thought happily. She now knew that Gideon did have a personal interest in her. His kiss that first night on the balcony had not been frivolous. It had meant something to him. An impulse perhaps, but not without some deeply felt purpose.

When Gideon returned home from yet another business trip to his head office in Sydney they had dinner together and he told Jessica that his translator would send her instalments of Luisa's diary as they were done each day. Her delight obviously gave Gideon pleasure and Jessica went to bed that night feeling even more convinced that he felt something very positive for her.

It was almost five o'clock the next afternoon when Professor Rex Anderson was ushered into the library by one of the staff. Jessica was startled and instantly apprehensive, realising that Rex would have received her response to his offer in the mail that morning. She had anticipated that her negative replies would frustrate him. She had not anticipated a personal visit.

She stood up slowly from her desk. 'Rex...did you want to see Mr Cavilha?' she prevaricated.

His eyes mocked her evasion. 'No. It's you I've come to see, Jessica...' he shot an impatient look at Doris, '...privately.'

'I was just about to pack up and go,' Doris said helpfully. 'If you don't mind putting my notes away, Jessica...'

'That's OK, Doris,' she nodded, resigning herself to the confrontation that Rex was obviously intent on forcing.

He said no more until Doris had left the library. Jessica noted that he had worn his best suit and was impeccably groomed. He was a handsome man, and very aware of it, Jessica suddenly realised, but not all the charm at his fingertips could soften her opinion of him now.

He walked over to where she stood, offering her the kind of smile that used to twist her heart. 'Jessica...' His voice throbbed with soft indulgence as he took her hands in his. His eyes projected warm understanding. 'I know it can only be hurt pride that made you write what you did. I came so that you could change your mind.'

'I'm not changing it, Rex,' she said firmly.

The smile faded. His eyes sharpened. 'Once you would have done anything for me, Jessica.'

She almost shuddered in revulsion at the memory of how she had let him use her. 'That time is past, Rex.'

He tried to find a chink in her armour against him. 'I love you, Jessica. Dawn was a brief aberration which I deeply regret. I know now that...'

'Rex, you don't love me. You don't love anyone,' Jessica cut in, impatient with his hypocrisy. 'You love, or not love, to suit your own convenience. Your own inclination. It's selfishness. Not love, Rex.'

Her cold indictment took him aback for a moment, but Jessica could see that his ego would not let him believe that she was now indifferent to him.

'Jessica, you have every reason to be upset. I treated you badly. But I assure you it will never happen again. We'll get married as soon as...'

'No!' She wrenched her hands out of his and put the length of the desk between them. 'I don't love you. I don't want to marry you. I don't even want to see you, ever again. It's over, Rex.'

His conciliatory manner dropped from him like a disposable cloak. His face grew stiff and his eyes flashed a deep resentment. 'It's Cavilha, isn't it? He took a fancy to you that afternoon in my office, and you think you can get to him. Well, let me tell you, you're off your brain if you think he'll ever marry you.'

Jessica disdained any reply to Rex's distortion of her relationship with Gideon. She stared stonily at her former lover, hating herself for ever having been duped by him.

He seemed to take her silence as encouragement for his voice suddenly switched to persuasive charm. 'Be sensible, Jessica. If you stay here you'll ruin yourself and your career. This project of Cavilha's is a wild-goose chase. Leave it. Come back and marry me.'

'I don't want to leave Pillatoro, and I don't want to marry you,' Jessica said flatly. 'I'm sorry you've given yourself this trip, but I could not have written more plainly to you. I don't want anything from you any more, Rex. I'd appreciate it if you'd leave now. We have nothing more to say to each other.'

His expression turned ugly as her words sank home. 'You think you can get away with that?' he demanded meanly. 'I'll get even with you, Jessica.'

'There's nothing to get even with,' Jessica retorted. 'I've never done anything to hurt you.'

'No one makes a fool of me. No one gets the better of me. I'll ...'

'Jessica . . .'

Gideon's voice stopped Rex dead. Jessica swivelled around to see Gideon framed in the doorway which led to his offices. She saw his expression change from one of anticipatory pleasure to that of stiff distaste as he caught sight of Rex.

'I beg your pardon. I didn't realise you had a visitor.' He nodded coldly to Rex. 'Professor Anderson.'

Sharp antagonism leapt across the space between the two men. Rex didn't bother to return Gideon's brief greeting. His gaze swept back to Jessica, stabbing vicious hatred at her. 'You'll regret this! Both of you,' he grated, then turned on his heel and strode out of the library.

Jessica shivered at the sheer venom of the man and Gideon quickly walked down the room, dropped the packet he had been holding on to her desk, and drew her into his arms. His eyes softly probed hers. 'What did he want, Jessica?'

She gave a cracked little laugh, unfreezing within the warmth of Gideon's embrace. 'He said he wanted to marry me.'

'And you refused?'

She nodded and drew in a deep breath, but she was unable to shake off a feeling of apprehension over Rex's threat. 'Gideon, he's a very vindictive man. He's got this idea . . . because you were comforting me that day you gave me the job . . . that . . . well, that you fancied me. And he thinks . . . He'll do us both an injury if he can, Gideon.'

'Empty words,' Gideon said with confidence.

Jessica was not so sure, but she did not pursue the subject. Gideon was holding her and that felt too good to let any thought of Rex spoil the moment. Her gaze lifted to his and suddenly there was not even a shadow of reserve in Gideon's eyes.

'Jessica...' Hope and need... a dark, pulsing need swirled down at her. 'It's really finished? You feel nothing for him now?' he asked, a harsh note of strained emotion in his voice.

'How could I?' she answered, unable to hide what she felt for him.

He sucked in a sharp breath. 'Then I wasn't mistaken that first night. We can...'

He didn't finish voicing his thought. His mouth came down on hers, seeking a more urgent confirmation of what she could share with him. At first his lips touched hers with exquisite tenderness, but her uninhibited response fired more pressing demands which quickly accelerated into an avid hunger for all she would give.

He pulled her closer, and Jessica could feel the passion rising in him and trembled from the sheer force of her own excitement. Gideon abruptly terminated the kiss and eased her away from him, his eyes still dark with passion, but urgently projecting reassurance.

'I know how deeply you've been hurt, Jessica, and I swear to you I won't do anything that might hurt you.'

'You could never hurt me, Gideon,' she whispered, her heart soaring with love for him.

He smiled, and his eyes were a dazzling bright blue. 'I hope I will always live up to the confidence you place in me.'

'You don't have to live up to anything,' she said happily.

He laughed, and Jessica had never seen him look so light-hearted. 'You don't know how good that sounds.' His face fell into more serious lines as he lifted one hand and gently stroked her cheek. 'Anderson wasn't wrong about my wanting you, Jessica. It's true that I was drawn to you that first day, but I didn't want to be. I tried to deny it to myself because it made me feel...disloyal to what I once had. But that first night here...it became something different. I felt...'

He sighed and a twist of irony curled his mouth. 'But then there was Sam.'

'Yes,' she murmured, more to herself than him, understanding the terrible conflict of interests.

The knowledge they shared pulsed between them, a deep bond of understanding that didn't need words. Gideon did want her. He hadn't spoken of love, but the need was very strong. Jessica was sure of that. She now began to believe that her dream could come true.

CHAPTER TEN

EACH day that passed brought a greater breadth and depth of understanding to their relationship. Jessica was content not to rush into a physical expression of their growing intimacy. That was only a matter of time, when it was right for both of them.

For one thing, there was the problem of Sam's sensibilities. Although Gideon made no mention of his brother's possible reaction to the situation, she knew he had to be concerned about it. Jessica was very conscious that Sam would surely find it painful to come home and see her with Gideon.

Meanwhile she worked on with the project, drawing up several new lines of investigation for Richard Cavilha's theory. It was almost a fortnight since Rex's visit and his scornful comment that she was working on a wild-goose chase, when Jessica was suddenly struck with the kind of inspiration that Gideon had wanted of her. Oddly enough it was not Richard Cavilha's notes that fired her mind along a new train of thought, but the translation of Luisa's diary.

It was after five o'clock when Luisa's maiden name struck a note of recognition. Sometimes surnames changed over generations. However unlikely, the possibilities kept pouring into Jessica's mind, forming a very definite shape that she had to follow.

Like a bloodhound on the scent she hunted up the list of archivists whom Richard Cavilha had employed and found the one she wanted. She quickly checked the time differences between Australia and Portugal, then booked a telephone call for eight o'clock that night. Her excitement was so great that she ran out to the parapet to see if she could spot Gideon's helicopter returning from his business trip to Sydney.

It was nowhere in sight and the wind was too strong for her to stay outside. There was a storm brewing. She hoped Gideon would not be caught out in it. He did not return in time for dinner, which was unusual. Of all days to be delayed it had to be this one, Jessica thought, her elation dimming somewhat because she could not share it with him. He was still not home when the call was put through at eight o'clock.

Fortunately the Portuguese archivist could speak English and he did not have to get an interpreter. He had some difficulty in understanding her accent and it took her an hour to explain what she wanted done, slowly repeating everything until she was sure her instructions were perfectly clear.

The sound of the beating helicopter-blades made her pulse leap. Gideon, home at last! The archivist had grasped all the essentials and it only took her a few more minutes to end the call. Even as she put the receiver down she was listening for Gideon's footsteps in the hall.

He had not yet come in although the helicopter had certainly landed. The engine had been shut off. The silence when that happened was overpowering. She hurried out through the great hall, impatient to see him and tell him what she had done. She thrust open the door and walked out to the archway, pausing there as a gust of wind swirled her skirt around her legs.

Gideon was nowhere in sight. The landing lights were still on. Two of the ground-staff were wheeling the helicopter towards the hangar at the back of the courtyard. The wind was making their task a little tricky. Jessica glanced up at the sky. There was not a star to be seen. The heavy blackness indicated that the storm was imminent. She was glad Gideon had got home before it broke.

'Mr Burrows,' she called out impulsively, 'is Mr Cavilha out there?'

The handyman yelled back some answer, but a howl of wind distorted the words. His wave towards the house seemed answer enough. Jessica frowned. Gideon had not come through the hall, but perhaps he had used the tradesmen's entrance, taking a short-cut to the kitchen to order a meal or whatever. She ran along the terrace and down the steps.

The kitchen was empty, the staff having retired for the night. She glanced up at the clock on the wall. It was past nine. A quick look in the small lounge and dining-room confirmed that Gideon was not in this part of the house. She hurried on, pausing on the octagonal floor below the great hall. Perhaps he had gone up to the music-room, or even to the library, seeking her.

The noise of a door banging at the end of the ballroom drew her attention. She walked around the fountain and spotted the opened door near the wall which faced the cliff-edge. The sharp gusts of wind and the following vacuum were driving it backwards and forwards. If it continued to slam like that the glass would break. Jessica ran down the length of the ballroom to secure the door before resuming her search for Gideon.

She was actually fastening the door when she saw him, a dark figure, darker than the blackness of the night which pressed around him. He stood at the furthest end of the cliff, arms leaning on the sandstone wall which was all that stood between him and the rock platform far below. Jessica's heart leapt into her mouth. What was he doing out there on so wild a night? She hastily reopened the door, stepped outside, and closed it firmly behind her. Why hadn't Gideon heard it banging?

The answer was obvious as she walked towards him. The howl of the wind and the crashing thunder of waves swept away any other sound. She saw Gideon sway, seemingly caught in the force of the elements, and fear gripped her throat. If he fell...the drop was so precipitous that nothing could save him. To her mind it was insanely reckless to be so close to the edge on such a night.

She shouted his name, but he gave no sign of hearing. Again she saw him sway, rocking on his feet. Fear for his safety overrode her own fear and she ran to him, grasping his arm. 'Come away from here, Gideon!' she cried urgently, trying to pull him back.

She might have been tearing at stone for all the effect she had on him, but his head slowly turned towards her. No muscle moved in his face. It was stamped with a cold control that nothing could reach, but the eyes held such a haunted, tortured look that Jessica instantly forgot where they were, the wildness of the wind, everything but Gideon's wretched suffering. Something was wrong. Terribly wrong.

'What is it?' she cried.

No response.

'Tell me!'

An enormous flash of lightning lit the sky. Jessica looked into eyes that did not even see her. The peal of thunder was like a death knell to all that their relationship had promised. He did not want her with him. He was locked back into his own world of inner pain and she was locked outside. But she could not go away. Could not leave him here.

'Gideon, please!' she begged despairingly.

Again he swayed. She wrapped her arms around his waist, instinctively protective. Lightning rent the clouds, almost directly above them, and Jessica cried out in fear. Gideon's arm moved, curving around her shoulders like an iron band.

'Jessica...' It was a breath of torment. 'Leave me. There's nothing you can do. Nothing anyone can do.' Harsh, hoarse words, torn from his throat and hunted by the wind.

'No! I won't leave you,' she gasped out determinedly. 'Tell me what's wrong. Tell me!'

He shook his head, then slowly turned his back to the sea, his gaze lifting, his face a strange mixture of love and anguish as his eyes drank in all that could be seen of Pillatoro. 'It's more than our home, Jessica. It's our tradition. And it's going to be taken away from us. All of it. The house and the grounds.'

'No!' It was a denial from her heart, as desperate as his bleak utterance. It couldn't be right. It made no sense.

She felt a shudder run through him and then at last he was turning towards her. The wind had torn strands of hair from her chignon and they whipped around her face. She saw his mouth curve in grim irony. One of his hands lifted to her hair, his fingers dislodging the pins as he tore the chignon loose.

'Just like that, Jessica,' he said with quiet ferocity as her hair came tumbling down. 'The whole structure...swept out from under us.'

'Pillatoro?' Still she couldn't believe it. Her whole body was rigid with shock. 'Who can take it away from you?'

A mirthless laugh broke from his throat and floated on the wind which swirled around them. His eyes glittered with a savage bitterness. 'The Government can. What they give, they can take away. They've amended the Wild Life and Parks Act to obtain the statutory right to reclaim it. The grounds will be left to return to their original state. The house will be turned into a local museum. For the use of the general public.'

'No! They can't do it! They can't!' The words tore off her tongue, her whole body pumping in violent upheaval. It would surely be the grossest act of vandalism, an act of terrible injustice against a family who had given more of itself to this country than any elected government.

'The compulsory acquisitions papers arrived at my Sydney office this morning.' Lightning crackled overhead and in its demonic glare of bluish light, Gideon's eyes swept the vast complex of Pillatoro with a feverish possessiveness. 'I'll demolish it, blow it up, anything rather than let it fall into their hands. It belongs to us. Every last stone built upon stone.'

It was no idle threat. The deep, riveting passion in his voice wrenched at Jessica's heart. 'It mustn't come to that. You must fight them, Gideon.'

'Fight them?' Again came that cracked, mirthless laugh. 'I've spent the day with Richard Pembroke who's the best lawyer in Sydney. The law can't do a thing! Tomorrow I'll be going to see the Minister for the Environment, but it's just going through the motions. The play is set. The end inevitable.'

'No! Don't say that!' She reached up and held his face, shaking it out of its rigidity. 'You'll find a way to stop them. You have to, Gideon.'

He looked down at her and for the first time since she had joined him at the parapet, his eyes really focused on her, burned into her with an agonising need. 'Jessica... there is no hope.'

'There's always hope,' she insisted passionately. 'Remember how hopeless it all seemed to Rafael and Luisa. You can't give up hope.' Her hands slid around his neck and she pressed her body to his, willing him to take strength from her as she had once received it from him. 'I won't let you give up hope, Gideon.' It was a wild thing to say, but every instinct had urged her to say it, just as every instinct clamoured to answer all his needs.

For a moment he tensed away from her. A gust of wind lifted her hair, billowing it out around him. He caught it in his hands, thrust it back on either side of her face, his palms flat against her ears. Another burst of lightning showed her the tortured loneliness in his eyes and she spoke with reckless haste, words spilling from her heart.

'Whatever you want of me is yours to have, Gideon. I know I haven't much of value to offer, but if it helps, I'm here for you. And always will be.'

His face suddenly twisted in pain. 'Now?' he asked hoarsely. 'Even now?'

Her fingers curled around his head, urging it down. 'More than ever now,' she whispered with urgent intensity, and pressed her mouth to his.

Their first kiss had been an exploration of a new world, a searching for knowledge, but Jessica no longer needed to search. She knew what was in her heart, and all the love and yearning she felt for Gideon flooded through her body, wanting to be transmitted to him.

She longed for his happiness with all her being, and anything she could give to assuage his pain was his to take. For the first time she could pour forth all these emotions, and her passionate offering was taken by Gideon with a hunger that was as wildly primitive as the storm which broke above them.

The wind howled. Thunder rumbled around them, an added drum-beat to the tumultuous crashing of the waves beneath them. Rain swept down in drenching gusts, but Jessica cared for nothing but Gideon. She held him tightly to her, knowing she would stand with him against all the force the elements had to offer, any force the world could wield.

Gideon dragged his mouth away. Even as he lifted his head back he thrust her body closer to his, hands running possessively over the slender curve of her hips and lower, pressing her into an intimate knowledge of his arousal. For long, throbbing moments his face was bared to the beat of the rain, chin raised in mute defiance of the storm raging around them.

Slowly, so slowly his head lowered, and his eyes mirrored the dark turbulence in his soul. 'I want all of you, Jessica. Nothing less would satisfy me.'

The vibrant intensity in his voice demanded no hesitation from her and she answered him with equal intensity. 'You have all of me, Gideon. For as long as I live.'

He lifted one hand, swept her hair aside and curled his fingers around the back of her neck. His chest heaved as he sucked in a quick breath. 'Do you know what you're saying?'

The hissed words held a strained urgency, as if he dared not let himself believe the commitment she had just given him, but a heady sense of freedom was singing through Jessica's heart. No longer did she have to hold back her emotions. She had revealed her love to him in words that no one could possibly misinterpret. 'Yes,' she answered in fervent affirmation. 'Yes.' And it was the sealing of a bond that could never be sundered.

Gideon might never come to love her as she loved him, but at this critical moment that was irrelevant. Answering his need was all-important. She arched her body closer to his, a gift already tuned to giving all that he wanted. His arms came around her, not merely accepting what she offered, but crushing her to him.

Their wet clothes were no barrier to the body-heat which pulsed from one to the other, fusing

strength to strength. She felt the surge of power
sweep through him, the indomitable will that would
never surrender easily to any fate. His voice
throbbed into her ear, no longer grim nor savage,
but fired with relentless purpose.

'We'll fight them, Jessica. We may not win, but
they'll remember for a long, long time the scars of
this battle.'

Elation soared through her veins. She had
brought him back from the brink of despair. She
pressed a smile to the strong pulse in his throat.
'Wherever you are I'll be with you,' she whispered.

He hugged her even more fiercely. His lips moved
through her hair, over her temples. 'And where I
sleep, will you be there, too?' he murmured with
tense passion.

'Yes,' she answered fervently, tilting her head
back to meet eyes which burnt into her soul.

His face held a wild, barbaric look. 'Until death
us do part?' he demanded.

'Yes,' she cried, caught up in the litany that was
older than the stones of Pillatoro, yet part of it,
part of Gideon, part of a promise which would
always hold true.

He laughed, a laugh of wild exultation. His hands
gripped her waist, almost spanning it as he lifted
her above his head, like a hostage to the storm that
raged around them. And he laughed up at her. 'Let
them do their worst!' Then he swung her down
against his chest, cradling her tightly to him. 'You
and I, Jessica. We'll stand against anything.'

'Yes,' she sang joyously, her heart thumping as
one with his as he strode out along the balcony,
carrying her with him.

Her wet skirt slapped against their legs. The wind lashed damp strands of hair around her face. She did not know where Gideon was taking her and she did not care. His arms held her to him in unrelenting possession and that was the only reality that mattered.

He flung a door open and Jessica caught only a glimpse of the bedroom before Gideon pushed through to an en suite bathroom. He switched on the light, lowered her feet to the floor and she looked up into a face which was no longer remote, no longer austere. His eyes were lit by an inner fire that burned into her flesh, into her very soul, building a heat that nothing could ever quench.

His hands came up and slowly undid the topmost button on her blouse. She trembled under their touch. 'You're cold,' he murmured, fingers moving quickly to rid her of the wet garment.

'No,' she whispered. 'It's what I've been waiting for all my life.'

His eyes lifted to hers, no longer probing, but softened into a haze of...something that Jessica had no knowledge of, but which moved her deeply...a compound of pleasure-pain that was threaded through with a need that encompassed her so totally that she instinctively reached out to him. Even as her fingers ran down his shirt, opening the buttons, exposing the firm breadth of his chest, Jessica knew she would do anything to assuage that need.

He eased the blouse from her body, down her arms, and then she was free to do the same for him.

She buried her face against his shoulder as she dragged the shirt-sleeves over his hands, and then his arms were around her, crushing her breasts against his body. For several moments they stood there, drugged by the sheer ecstasy of this first naked contact, hearts thumping in wild palpitation.

Then Gideon took a towel and started to dry her back. The sensuous touch of the warm, fluffy material caressing her skin made Jessica shiver. It moved to her shoulders and Gideon tilted her away from him. He took her breasts in both hands, gently drying them with the towel, and the slow eroticism of the movement fanned ripples of pleasure that had Jessica gasping for breath. Gideon's mouth came down on hers, no longer seeking but owning with a passion that took all that she offered, and never in her life had Jessica felt so possessed.

When his head slowly lifted from hers, she stared up at him with mesmerised eyes, totally his to do with as he wished. She could not read the expression on his face. It was not elation. It was not triumph. There was an amalgam of expectation and some hidden emotion which lay far deeper, feeding an uncertainty that stabbed at her heart. That he should feel any doubt was beyond bearing at this moment.

'What is it?' she asked, her voice thick and furred with emotion.

'I don't want to hurt you. Not in any way. Are you sure, Jessica?'

The softly spoken question begged an answer that would last a lifetime, and she gave it. 'You could never hurt me, Gideon. Not any more. Not ever.'

She pressed close again and felt the light shudder that ran through him as he released his breath in a long sigh. His hands reached for the zipper of her skirt and she was only too ready to step out of her clothes when he thrust them down. He reached for the belt of his trousers but Jessica forestalled him.

'No. Let me do that for you, Gideon,' she said quietly, and revelled in the opportunity of touching him as he had touched her, loving every finely honed muscle of his beautiful male body.

'Oh, God!' The groan was torn from his throat as he pulled her to him.

He clutched her against him with a rough urgency as he strode into the bedroom, and then he was laying her on his bed, taking her in his arms, lifting her body to his. There was no hesitation, no evasion, no doubts. They were one in a passion so total, so immense that it obliterated all other existence and the only life was that pulsing between them, in them, around them, building to its own intrinsic fulfilment, a timeless time of unforgettable oneness.

Outside, the storm lashed itself violently against the coast, but its fury aroused no fear in Jessica. She knew a peace that nothing could touch. It was as if the whole purpose of her life had been consummated this night, and whatever the future, no one could take this away from her.

The heartbeat beneath her ear was even and gentle, the sound feathered by the soft rise and fall of Gideon's chest. A smile of utter contentment curved Jessica's mouth. He was at peace, too. Her hand roved over his body, rediscovering and renewing the pleasure of touching him freely: the muscular breadth of his shoulders, the lean strength of his hips, the long, powerful thighs. Everything about him was so right, so beautiful.

More than once he stirred under the lightness of her touch, arms tightening, holding her even closer to him, his legs shifting to entwine with hers, instinctively clinging on to their oneness. And joy swelled the fullness of Jessica's heart. Gideon did not want to let her go. He no more wanted separation than she did.

He had not spoken any words of love to her. Words had seemed unnecessary, out of place within the context of their coming together. The fierce act of mutual possession had transcended any other communication, and the feeling of completeness was too overwhelming for any question to be raised.

His fingers entwined themselves in her hair as if he would bind her to him in every way possible. And then he spoke. 'There's something I have to tell you, Jessica.'

There was a tense undertone in his voice that sent a ripple of apprehension over Jessica's contentment. She sensed his hesitation, felt his reluctance to continue.

'Go on,' she urged, needing to know even if the knowledge hurt her.

'One thing I found out yesterday...' Again he paused, and his fingers curled around her head, pressing it to his heart. 'The advice to the Minister to take over Pillatoro came from the chairman of the Cultural and Heritage Commission.'

Rex!

Rex . . . wreaking his vicious revenge . . . getting even.

It was because of her that Gideon's home was threatened! Because of her . . .

CHAPTER ELEVEN

'IT'S not your fault any more than it's mine, so don't think it is, Jessica,' Gideon commanded with tense urgency.

'But it is,' she cried despairingly. 'If you hadn't met me...'

'If I hadn't met you I'd never have known what we have now. And faced with the choice, I'd give up Pillatoro before I'd lose what you give me,' he said with such intense passion that Jessica was awed by his feeling for her. 'But we're not going to surrender passively, and I'll be damned if we'll give it up,' he continued just as passionately. 'One way or another, Anderson is not going to win. And if you let yourself think it's your fault, Jessica, he's already won. What we've got to do is work out how to win the war, because that's what we'll give them. Total war.'

The terrible burden of guilt which had dropped on to her heart lifted. Gideon was right. They had to look forward, not backward. What was done was done. Somehow they had to foil Rex's vindictive checkmate. Despite what Gideon had said, Jessica felt he could never be fully happy anywhere else but here. It had been bred into him. She would never forget the despair she had seen in him, out there on the parapet.

'If it can help, you can use my... my affair with Rex to show up bad faith on his part, Gideon,' she offered, uncaring of the humiliation that would mean for herself so long as it could help Gideon in any way.

'No! I won't have you hurt. Not for any reason.'

'But if we expose Rex's bias . . . get the media to reveal the personal background . . .' she argued.

'Can't be done, anyhow. There is a law of libel, Jessica. Anderson has a good professional reputation, which is why I went to him in the first place. He'd easily weather any mud thrown at him.'

'But, Gideon . . .' She struggled up out of his hold. It was too dark to see his expression but she laid her head next to his on the pillow and he turned his face towards her. 'Surely the media could help in some way to publicise the case from a sympathetic angle. People don't like the Government taking things over, especially a family home. If we could get popular opinion on our side . . .'

Gideon suddenly chuckled. 'How right you are,' he said with relish. 'I'll see Hal Chissolm first thing in the morning. We were at school together and have been friends ever since. He and his father will throw the whole Chissolm media empire behind us. The Government might have us on a point of law, but by God, there'll be some other points made before we get to the Supreme Court.'

Jessica knew of the Chissolms. They controlled many newspapers and two television channels as well. It did not surprise her that Gideon should be closely connected to people of power and influence. Her mind was busily searching for more helpful suggestions when Gideon spoke again.

'I'll have to be in Sydney tomorrow, but you could organise all the material that might be helpful, Jessica. I want you to go through all the documents relating to Pillatoro. Doris will show you where they're kept. Family history, every part a Cavilha has played for this country. It may serve no purpose, but we don't know yet what may or may not be important. Hal might be able to use it in some effective way.'

'You know that will mean the loss of privacy, Gideon,' she warned, thinking of the tragic deaths of his family which were still so close to him. She hesitated, then softly asked, 'Are you prepared to use everything?'

His hand lifted and caressed her cheek. 'There is a time to protect and a time to lay everything bare. You taught me that tonight. We won't hold back. Not now.'

He kissed her with a tenderness that made Jessica feel as though she was very precious to him, and for a long time they held each other tightly, locking out the hostile world. Their hearts and minds throbbed with a unity of purpose that no force could ever separate.

'What about Sam, Gideon?' Jessica finally asked. 'He'll want to fight too.'

'Yes.' Gideon sighed. 'There's nothing Sam would relish more than a head-on confrontation, but that wouldn't achieve anything.'

'He is an international star, someone Australians are proud of. Couldn't something be made out of that?' Jessica suggested hopefully.

'The Melbourne concert! Of course! It's to be a national telecast and it's the perfect showcase for Sam to make a point. I'll speak to him about it tomorrow.'

They talked far into the night, tossing around ideas until they could think of no more. Jessica fell asleep, still cradled in Gideon's arms. She awoke to the touch of a hand lightly stroking her hair. The grey light of early morning showed her Gideon already shaved and dressed in a sober business suit. He leaned over and kissed her.

'I must go now, Jessica,' he said regretfully. 'I don't know when I'll be back. Hold the fort for me,' he added with a faint smile that affirmed the understanding they had forged last night.

'You have only to tell me and I'll do whatever you ask,' she said huskily, wishing he had woken her earlier.

'I know,' he murmured. 'Thank you, Jessica.'

And there was a wealth of meaning in those few words. He did not say goodbye and Jessica knew that there never would be a goodbye said by either of them. Even when he left her and the door closed behind him, she was with him wherever he went, wherever he was. Their lives had been joined last night and although Gideon might never see her as a woman he wanted to marry, she was a part of him that would never be discarded. What was his, he held, as he would hold Pillatoro. Or destroy it.

But it mustn't ever come to that, Jessica thought fiercely, swinging her legs out of bed in her eagerness to begin the task Gideon had given her. She retrieved her still wet clothes from Gideon's bathroom, wrapped a towel around her nakedness and dashed down the passageway to her own room. She had just stepped into the shower when she heard the helicopter engine start up. Her heart lurched a little then steadied into a strong, purposeful beat as she held on to the sense of togetherness.

Within half an hour of Gideon's leaving, Jessica was in the library, immersing herself in the private papers of the Cavilha family. Gideon had told her much of the tragedies that had overtaken his family, but still the obituary lists appalled her.

The Cavilha men had died across the world in the strange places where people had fought and died. The First World War had been particularly deadly. The names loomed out of the private letters and obituary records... Gallipoli, Ypres, Pozières, St Quentin. The mentions in despatches, the medals for bravery did nothing to alleviate the sadness of so much promising life wasted.

The Second World War was the same. Richard Cavilha's two brothers had died; one in the battleship *Canberra* off Guadalcanal, the other at El Alamein, neither of them having married. And so it had come down to Richard and Rebecca to breathe the next life into Pillatoro, Gideon and Samson, the last survivors of a line which should have been so prolific.

Doris arrived for work along with the rest of the clerical staff and Jessica did not hesitate to use the authority Gideon had given her. She called a meeting, explained the crisis facing them all, and then set special tasks for everyone. All the Cavilhas' charity bequests were to be listed, every kind of employment the family had provided had to be enumerated, the grants given to medical research, academic research, other special causes.

She overlooked nothing in her zeal to prepare any line of defence that Gideon might be able to use,

and the staff responded with a zeal born of the same
outrage she felt. She was not surprised at the loyalty
that Gideon and Pillatoro had inspired in them. To
her it was entirely natural, and no one raised the
slightest question about her authority to organise
the work she had put into process. The library
became the war-room where all the information was
gathered and sifted and placed in piles of
importance.

It was just past two o'clock when Gideon telephoned to say that Hal Chissolm was on his way
to Pillatoro with a news team. Gideon himself was
on his way to another meeting with Richard Pembroke and Jessica quickly agreed to give the media
men every co-operation. Even this short, impersonal conversation seemed wonderfully intimate to
Jessica, confirming yet again Gideon's trust in her
and her judgement.

The news team arrived in their own helicopter
and Jessica met them in the courtyard. She had no
trouble picking out Hal Chissolm. He carried the
same innate air of strength and authority that was
so much a part of Gideon's character. He was tall
and dark, lean of face and body, with a hard,
ruthless cut about him. Silver-grey eyes assessed her
sharply, even as he offered her a smile of greeting.
He had three other men with him, a newspaper editor and two reporters whom he introduced without
preamble.

'Gideon said you were in charge of all the family
records,' Hal Chissolm prompted.

'Yes. I've organised various categories of data
which might be of help to you,' Jessica answered.

'It's all set out in the library if you'll accompany me.'

They settled around her desk and listened respectfully as she summarised what was in the records in front of her. With the trained instinct of a good researcher she honed in on the points which might best win public support for the cause, and it gave her considerable private satisfaction to see the cool speculation in Hal Chissolm's eyes gradually change to warm approval. His smile when she finished speaking held more than approval and the grey eyes glinted with quiet triumph.

'Thank you, Miss Trelawney. You've given us the line we need.' The other men looked at him expectantly and he swept them with an authoritative glance. 'In the immortal words of John F. Kennedy, "Ask not what your country can do for you, but what you can do for your country." The Cavilha story embodies that sentiment and that's how we'll put it to the public.' He suddenly grinned. 'Makes the Government case look hopelessly mean to be pulling the mat out from such a family, wouldn't you say?'

Jessica could not help grinning back at him in agreement. 'I'd say.'

He turned to his newspaper editor. 'Right, Charlie?'

'Got you,' the man nodded. 'OK if we take photocopies of some of these documents, Miss Trelawney?'

'Yes, of course. Any of the staff here will help you with whatever you want.'

She moved aside as Charlie and his two men huddled around the desk. Hal Chissolm took her

arm and led her away. 'Come. I want you to show
me through Pillatoro, and give me all the background history. Tomorrow I'll be back with a television crew to shoot a film on it for our current
affairs programme, and I want to plot out an effective sequence tonight.'

Jessica complied, giving him all that she had read
and all that Gideon had told her. Hal Chissolm's
interest was particularly caught by the story of the
stained-glass window, the music-room and the
portrait of Rebecca Magee, and even more particularly by the schoolroom with its wall of paintings
by all the Cavilha children.

They returned to the library. By the time Hal and
his men had finished collecting the material they
wanted it was past five o'clock, and the staff made
their departure with them. Jessica wondered how
Gideon had fared with his meetings in Sydney and
hoped he would be pleased with what she had done
to hold the fort.

It was past nine o'clock when Gideon telephoned
again, and Jessica felt a surge of warm pleasure as
she listened to his voice relating his own and Hal
Chissolm's appreciation of her work.

'Are there any new developments, Gideon?' she
asked as soon as he paused.

'We've decided to take out a restraining in-
junction which Pembroke will argue in court.
Probably at the end of this week. Sam is preparing
a statement of his own for the concert tomorrow
night. We're doing all we can to bring influence to
bear on the Government to reverse its position
but...' He sighed. 'It's been a long day, and I'm

still at a meeting. Goodnight, Jessica. Sleep well,' he added softly.

'And you,' she murmured huskily, longing for the intimacy of last night, and knowing that he could not be with her tonight.

The next day was even more demanding on everyone. The story of the Government's resumption claim on Pillatoro was broken in the morning newspapers. Other reporters arrived, seeking interviews and stories. Hal's television crew had to be protected from interruption. Jessica was kept so busy, she had little time for any more detailed study of the Cavilha records.

Every television channel carried stories on the Cavilha family that night, and the programme Hal had shaped for his current affairs show carried tremendous emotional impact. Then, just an hour later, came the charity concert in Melbourne, televised nationally, and Sam held centre stage in all his imposing greatness, his red hair and beard shining brightly above the stark black dinner-suit, his magnificent voice rolling out to an audience far greater than that packed into the theatre.

'Tonight I have chosen to sing for you Mahler's "Songs of a Wayfarer". The professional schedule of an opera-singer forces one into becoming something of a wayfarer, but I have always been proud to call Australia home. It was always a comfort to know that my family home, Pillatoro, was here, waiting for my return.'

He paused to add more emphasis to his next words, injecting them with a note of ineffable sadness. 'However, it now seems that my Government sees fit to take our home away from my family who built it over a century ago and have lived there and loved it ever since. Should it be lost to us, then I shall indeed be a wayfarer, so you know that tonight I sing from the heart.'

And he did, his voice a vehicle of such passionate need and longing that tears welled into Jessica's eyes and trickled down her cheeks unheeded. Even when his performance finished the audience was still in thrall for several long, silent moments before erupting into a standing ovation. Sam did not bow. He simply stood there, striking a figure of lonely dignity while wave after wave of almost frenzied applause pleaded for him to stay. Finally the theatre hushed into an expectant silence.

Sam's voice throbbed out, an instrument of poignant regret. 'It has always been a great pleasure to perform in front of my home-people. Thank you. God bless you all.'

Then he bowed and walked from the stage with an air of finality which choked any thought of applause. The implication of his speech had been perfectly clear. If Pillatoro was taken, then Australia would no longer be his home and no more would he grace an Australian stage. No threat had been spoken, no accusation, no blistering rhetoric against injustice, yet the well of sympathy he had stirred was almost a tangible thing.

Intermission followed immediately upon Sam's departure, which was a stroke of superb planning on someone's part, since any act which followed Sam's would have been an anticlimax. Jessica suspected that it had been Sam's hand behind the programming, purposely leaving the audience with a ready-made subject to discuss during the interval.

As a public relations exercise to favour the Cavilha family home, the day could only be counted a resounding success, but there was no note of triumph in Gideon's voice when he telephoned Jessica a few minutes after Sam's performance. He sounded tired as he told her the court hearing was set for tomorrow afternoon and that Sam would be flying up to Sydney for it to lend any weight he could to their cause.

Jessica knew how much would depend upon the judge's decision. 'I want to be there with you, Gideon,' she said impulsively.

There was a long pause. 'Jessica . . .'

Her heart beat a tattoo of love as she heard the note of longing in his voice.

' . . . I'll send the helicopter for you. Can you be ready in half an hour?'

'Yes,' she said without hesitation.

A little over an hour later, Jessica arrived at the Regent Hotel. A chauffeur-driven limousine had been waiting for her at the helipad. A porter was waiting at the hotel steps to carry her overnight bag. Even a lift was being held open to whisk her straight up to Gideon's executive suite.

It seemed like a lifetime ago since she had been here, waiting in this very hotel for Gideon to pick her up and take her to Pillatoro . . . the centre of his world. The irony of the situation struck deep. Now Gideon was waiting for her, and if he lost Pillatoro tomorrow, Jessica was afraid that she could never compensate him for the loss. It would haunt them all their lives.

Gideon opened the door to her. He dismissed the porter with a handsome tip and then he was drawing

Jessica into his embrace, almost crushing her against him, his mouth sweeping over her hair in a mute expression of need and relief. 'I've missed you,' he rasped.

They did not talk. They communed with their bodies, need answering need with a compulsion that held an edge of desperation. Tomorrow would inevitably come, but for several long hours they sought forgetfulness of what tomorrow would bring, clinging to each other, firing passion and soothing it, and eventually slipping into a sleep of utter exhaustion.

CHAPTER TWELVE

'WHAT exactly is the case being argued this afternoon, Gideon?' Jessica asked him over breakfast the next morning.

He had been silent and tense, listening to the news on the radio and checking the newspapers ever since they had risen. His face was grimly austere, and his eyes murderous coals of frustration as he answered her.

'The Government will argue that beyond its local curiosity value, Pillatoro has no historical standing which would count as national heritage. This allows the property and the buildings to be brought under the Wild Life and Parks Act. Professor Anderson is their expert witness and his professional opinion is their evidence.'

'So, you have to prove that it does have historical value.'

'That's about the size of it. Pembroke will be here soon to go over my testimony with me.' His expression softened as he perceived Jessica's distress over Rex's perfidy. 'It's all we can do now, Jessica.'

She nodded. 'Maybe if I testified for you, with my qualifications I could...'

'No. There's nothing you can say that I can't, and I wouldn't put you through the ordeal of being cross-examined, Jessica. Not with Anderson in court.'

Jessica knew Gideon was right. He knew the history of Pillatoro better than she did, and her qualifications and professional standing were no match for Rex's. She did not argue. All she could give Gideon now was her moral support.

Richard Pembroke arrived shortly after nine o'clock. The QC cut a handsome figure of a man, tall, broad-shouldered, the sprinkle of grey in his dark hair adding to his distinguished air. He took Jessica's hand gravely as Gideon introduced her, grey eyes measuring her mettle.

'I'm very pleased to meet you, Miss Trelawney,' he said in a deep, beautifully modulated voice. 'I understand you've been organising the publicity. And very effectively, too. If there's any relevant point we miss this morning, please don't hesitate to give your view. Gideon tells me you're well qualified in historical research.'

They sat down. Jessica listened intently as the barrister rehearsed questions and answers with Gideon, but there was nothing she could add to the testimony. When the telephone rang, Gideon silently gestured for her to answer it and Jessica was surprised to hear Doris Mavin's voice on the line.

'Jessica, a telex has come in from Portugal. I don't know if it's important right now, but I thought I'd better tell you.'

From Portugal! The project had completely slipped Jessica's mind since the crisis over Pillatoro itself had arisen, but if her inspiration had borne fruit... excitement suddenly pumped through her heart. 'Read it to me, Doris.'

'It says—"Your assumption re diary and contents proved correct. Photostats to follow. Congratulations on inspiration. Richard Cavilha would have been proud of you. Paul Riviera." That's all, Jessica.'

'That's enough, Doris,' she said exultantly. 'Thanks a million.'

She put the telephone down and turned to Gideon, a smile of huge relief on her face. 'We've got the proof! Your father's project, Gideon. There's a historical link between Pillatoro and the first discovery of the East Coast of Australia. In all the worry about this, I forgot to tell you what I'd done about the project.'

Both Gideon and Richard Pembroke were puzzled by her triumphant claim, but listened with growing understanding as Jessica poured out an explanation of what had been found in Portugal.

'That's it then,' the QC declared with satisfaction. 'This will blow the Government's case out of court. All we have to do is put Miss Trelawney in the witness-box and her testimony will clinch it.'

Gideon frowned. 'Is that necessary? Surely I can testify for her.'

Richard Pembroke shook his head. 'It's Miss Trelawney's research. She is the professional in this field. We have to have expert knowledge to counter any arguments thrown up by Professor Anderson.'

Jessica lightly squeezed Gideon's arm, loving him for his protective concern, but knowing that this was something she had to do for him. 'It's all right, Gideon. I'm happy to do it.'

Richard Pembroke immediately switched to the task of rehearsing Jessica's testimony.

Jessica was suddenly very glad that she had thought to wear the blue linen suit she had bought for professional meetings. The tailored outfit was softened by a white silk blouse which featured a feminine floppy bow at its neckline. She had carefully coiled the thick mass of her hair around her crown and pinned it securely, anxious that it stay sleek and tidy all day. At least she looked professional, she thought, trying to quell the flock of butterflies in her stomach. She hoped she would sound professional, too.

Sam arrived. Gideon quickly briefed him on the new development while the barrister worked on with Jessica, meticulously going over and over the facts. Sam came forward, taking Jessica's hands, his eyes warmer than ever with admiration for her.

'I knew Pillatoro needed you. Thank you, Jessica,' he said simply, but his voice carried a depth of feeling that embarrassed her.

Jessica instantly resolved to tell Sam the truth about her feelings for Gideon once the court-case was over. He had the right to know. She hoped that the relief of having won the case would mitigate the hurt she could not avoid inflicting.

Hal Chissolm dropped in for a while. Other people came and went, quiet-voiced clerks and aides who delivered and took papers away with them. An early lunch was served in the suite. Bernadette and her parents arrived.

'I thought you might like to have Bernadette sit next to you in the court-room, Jessica,' Gideon murmured to her after he had introduced Mr and Mrs Adriani. His eyes searched hers anxiously for one private moment. 'Have I asked too much of you?'

'No,' she whispered. 'Don't worry about me. I'll be all right. Thanks for thinking of Bernadette.'

He sighed, relaxing a little. 'Sam and I have to be with Pembroke. When this is over...'

Richard Pembroke called him aside, interrupting whatever Gideon had been going to say, and there were no more private moments. Very soon afterwards they all left for the law courts and Jessica rode in the Adrianis' car. She was glad of Bernadette's sympathetic company and liked the girl's parents, who volubly expressed their hope that the Government would drop its action. She felt a warm aura of support as they accompanied her into the courtroom where the legal process would take place.

The cold, formal furnishings of the law struck a chord of fear in Jessica. The publicity about the case had attracted many reporters and the room was filled with interested spectators long before the judge made his entrance. Jessica had seen Rex Anderson arrive, but she resolutely ignored his presence. The arguments began and Jessica listened intently to every word, admiring the skill of Richard Pembroke in his role of barrister, and resenting the points made by the opposing counsel.

When Rex Anderson was called to the witness-box, Jessica brought all her concentration to bear on his answers. The charm and confidence of the man were all too apparent, and his assured manner carried conviction. On the rare occasions he glanced towards Gideon and Jessica, his eyes glinted with triumph.

Richard Pembroke tried to goad him into an admission of his bias against the Cavilhas, but Rex was too slippery to be caught. He kept making the point that Pillatoro was an anachronism, established long before proper planning of the national parks became effective. The Cavilhas had had it for over a hundred years. That was long enough. Now it should be restored to its rightful owners, the Australian people. Richard Pembroke could not break him. His last question was:

'Professor Anderson, in your professional opinion, does Pillatoro have any historical value that would only be preserved if the Cavilhas were to stay living there?'

Rex's eyes caught Jessica's and his smile was almost gloating. 'Outside its own limited area, none whatsoever,' he declared decisively.

Gideon was sitting just in front of her and she saw his back straighten and tense. She mentally consigned Rex Anderson to hell for all eternity for the grief he was determined on inflicting. When Richard Pembroke called her to the witness-box she walked past Professor Anderson with scornful dignity, disdaining even to glance in his direction.

She was sworn in and the barrister took her through a statement of her qualifications. Then he began on the evidence they had rehearsed as preliminary groundwork to the critical thrust of her testimony. The substance of it was to show that, contrary to Rex Anderson's opinion, Pillatoro did have a historical interest which would be destroyed if the Cavilhas were dispossessed of their home.

She concentrated on how it was a symbol of what Rafael, a poor Portuguese immigrant, had

achieved; how generation after generation of Cavilhas had fought to protect it; how to deprive them
of their home would be an act of historical vandalism. She could feel the interest she was creating,
and even Justice Legge asked her a couple of questions which suggested she had struck a chord of
sympathy in him.

The disconcerted look on Rex Anderson's face
gave her a quiet pleasure. He and the Government
barrister were whispering heatedly as Richard Pembroke drew her out about the research project which
was the introduction to the final, clinching
argument.

'Now, Miss Trelawney, will you please tell the
court about the discovery that has just been made
in Portugal.'

For the first time since she had ascended the
witness-box, Jessica looked directly at Gideon, her
heart overflowing with love for him. The evidence
she would now give was for him, for his father, for
Pillatoro. 'I received word this morning that a Portuguese archivist, Paul Riviera, has found the secret
diary of Christovel Mendonca, the first man to dis-
cover and explore the East Coast of Australia.'

The instant buzz around the court gave rise to a
call for order. Justice Legge peered over his glasses
at Jessica. 'That is not in any history book of mine,
my dear.'

'The diary has only just been found, Your
Honour. Its historical significance may well be
argued for a generation, but there is a great deal
of circumstantial evidence in existence to support
its claims. The history books may have to be re-
written. The point I wish to make here is that the
diary was found at the home where Luisa Cavilha's

parents once lived. Luisa was a direct descendant of Christovel Mendonca.'

Another buzz went around the courtroom and again came the call for order. Jessica took a deep breath and continued. 'Richard Cavilha traced the family link between Luisa and Mendonca. I made the assumption that when Luisa eloped with Rafael and came to Australia, this country would become anathema to Luisa's parents. This was in fact what happened. All references to Mendonca's Pacific voyages were locked away, never to be referred to again.'

Her voice rang out firmly as she gave her conclusive argument. 'If Mendonca's diary is accepted by historians as historical fact, then Pillatoro has a direct link with the first discovery of Australia by white people. Any government that disturbed that link in order to increase its area of national parks would be completely irresponsible in my professional opinion. This is evidence that the Minister has not taken into account when making his decision. He could not, since it has only just been found.'

Rex was still hissing at the Government barrister, but Jessica knew he could do nothing about this new development. A wave of triumph rippled through her. She had done it. She had saved Pillatoro for Gideon.

'Thank you, Miss Trelawney,' Richard Pembroke said with a rich note of satisfaction. 'That will be all.'

'I have a few questions for Miss Trelawney,' his opposing counsel drawled, rising to his feet.

Richard Pembroke raised a sceptical eyebrow, waved a half-mocking invitation, and sat down with the air of a man whose case was well and truly won.

Jessica looked enquiringly at the other barrister who waited for absolute silence before he spoke. His eyes bored into Jessica's; cold, cold eyes, full of deadly purpose. When he spoke, it was in a loud, contemptuous tone.

'Miss Trelawney, have you had sexual relations with Professor Anderson?'

The question shook Jessica. It was totally unexpected and horribly shaming. She could feel the blood draining from her face and she clenched her hands tightly as she fought for control over her reeling mind.

Richard Pembroke was on his feet, protesting vigorously. 'Your Honour, I object to this line of questioning. It has absolutely no relevance to the case in question.'

'On the contrary, Your Honour, I intend to show that Miss Trelawney is biased and without integrity, and her evidence is worthless and must be thrown out of court.'

Jessica felt as if an iron fist had closed around her heart and was squeezing it unmercifully. She had not expected this type of personal malevolence from Rex. Not in a public court. She realised now that he would break her if he could. Through his spokesman.

'Go ahead, but be very careful, Mr Garrick,' Justice Legge enjoined drily.

The question was repeated. Even more forcefully and scathingly. Jessica could not bear to look at Sam or Bernadette, and particularly not at Gideon.

Somehow she found the same serene composure
that had descended on her that dreadful day in the
library when she had had to confront Gideon about
his father's theory. She lifted her chin, faced her
prosecutor squarely, folded her hands on her lap
and spoke with quiet dignity.

'Yes.'

'Have you had sexual relations with Mr Gideon
Cavilha?'

Both Richard Pembroke and Gideon leapt to
their feet. The legal squabbling went on. Mr Garrick's strident voice punched out the critical argument. 'I will prove this woman to be completely
unscrupulous, Your Honour.'

The question was allowed. It was repeated. Flung
at her.

'Yes,' she whispered.

'Speak up, Miss Trelawney. The court can't hear
you,' Mr Garrick insisted.

'Yes.'

She saw the look of shock which passed over
Bernadette's face. She cringed inwardly at the pain
she must inadvertently be giving Sam. But most of
all her heart bled for Gideon, knowing how he
would hate this public exposure of his private
affairs.

'You make a practice of sleeping with your employers in order to further your career?' Mr Garrick
continued with relentless purpose.

'No.'

'But you have only had two employers and you've
slept with both of them.'

'Yes.'

'Very interesting. Do you profess to love Mr Gideon Cavilha?'

'I don't profess to. I do love him.'

'And you'd do anything for him, would you not?'

'Yes.'

'Even to fabricating evidence to save Pillatoro for your lover?'

'No. I wouldn't do that. Without integrity, love is worthless.'

'Exactly. I suggest that your love for Gideon Cavilha is without integrity and completely worthless. Aren't all your schemes and stratagems designed to make yourself mistress of Pillatoro?'

Jessica closed her eyes and shook her head.

'You must answer, Miss Trelawney,' Justice Legge instructed.

She looked up at him with pained eyes. He was no longer smiling at her, no longer looking indulgently at her. She turned to her persecutor and forced herself to speak. 'No, that's not true.'

'Come now, Miss Trelawney. You expect to marry Mr Gideon Cavilha. Marry into Pillatoro.'

'No, I don't expect that.'

'Miss Trelawney, you slept with Professor Anderson and expected to marry him. Is that not so?'

Her eyes moved to Rex, meeting his gloating gaze with bitter contempt. 'Professor Anderson and I did have that understanding at one time.'

'And now you live under the same roof as Mr Gideon Cavilha. You've slept with him. And you want us to believe you have no expectations of marrying him?'

The question was loaded with blistering scorn for her assertion, but Jessica faced the barrister squarely, an innate pride in her own integrity giving strength to her voice. 'No. I do not expect anything of Mr Gideon Cavilha, nor has he promised me anything.'

Surprise flitted across the hard, sharp face of her adversary, but his voice brimmed with sarcasm. 'So, on the one hand you say you love Gideon Cavilha, you've slept with him, but you have no expectations of marrying him. Unbelievable! I say you are a liar, Miss Trelawney. I say that all your actions and statements are based on your desire to marry into the family, and your historical defence of Pillatoro is motivated by prejudice and is totally unreliable. All your evidence is based on self-concern. Is that not so, Miss Trelawney?'

Jessica shook her head helplessly under the continuing barrage. 'No. No to all you've said.' Tears pricked her eyes and she glanced pleadingly at Richard Pembroke, but he was not looking at her. His head was bent towards Sam and he was listening intently to whatever Sam was saying.

Mr Garrick's voice hammered on. 'Your Honour, I submit that Miss Trelawney will sleep with anyone who will further her ambitions, and say anything that will further her interests. I submit that her evidence should be discarded as worthless, biased and prejudicial.' He half-bowed to the judge and swept back to his seat, almost insolently confident.

'Your Honour...'

Jessica dragged her gaze back to Richard Pembroke who had risen to his feet.

'...this most scurrilous attack upon Miss Trelawney's character and integrity can be easily refuted. No one here can doubt the truthfulness of this witness. She has laid herself bare before the court. I shall ask Miss Trelawney only three questions, Your Honour, and the answers to those questions will prove that all Mr Garrick's insinuations are completely unfounded.'

He turned to Jessica, walked towards her, smiling. His eyes were kind, sympathetic, encouraging. He leaned his arm on the witness-box, half-turning towards the court so that his voice wooed every listener. 'Miss Trelawney, did Samson Cavilha ask you to marry him?'

Jessica looked at Samson, who returned her gaze steadily, apparently unconcerned about baring his soul to the public. She looked past him at Bernadette whose face had turned ashen. Oh God! Where does it end? she thought miserably. She could bear her own reputation being torn to shreds, but Gideon and Sam and Bernadette were all suffering from what she was being forced to say.

'Miss Trelawney, you must answer,' Richard Pembroke insisted gently.

'Yes,' she answered sadly.

'Did he offer Pillatoro to you as your home for the rest of your life?'

'Yes.'

'What reason did you give for refusing his offer of marriage and Pillatoro?'

Jessica looked at Sam through a blur of tears. 'Samson Cavilha is a great man, a good man, but I do not love him as a man such as he is deserves to be loved,' she choked out, then bent her head as the tears overflowed and trickled down her cheeks.

'Your Honour, if this woman had wanted to be mistress of Pillatoro, she could have achieved that position very easily with just one word. But being a woman of the utmost integrity, she didn't speak that very simple little word. If Your Honour is still in any doubt on the matter, I could call a number of witnesses who will swear on oath that Miss Trelawney put her job as a historical researcher on the line over a point of integrity which she insisted upon, even when threatened with dismissal by Mr Gideon Cavilha.'

'Thank you, Mr Pembroke, but I don't think we need waste any more of the court's time. You have made your point,' Justice Legge declared roundly, then dropped his voice to a gentler tone. 'You may stand down now, Miss Trelawney.'

Richard Pembroke grasped her arm as she emerged from the witness-box. She felt completely numb, dreadfully exposed and hopelessly vulnerable. The barrister was leading her back to her seat before Jessica's mind clicked into feverish action. She could not bear to stay in this courtroom where she had been shamed beyond endurance. She could not bear to face Bernadette or Sam. And the last thing Gideon would want or need was to be associated with her now.

She saw Gideon stand up. Sam rose also. Of course they would stand by her. That was the kind of men they were. But she did not want them to. She could not bear their... their charity. Half blinded by tears and uncaring of what anyone thought, she broke into a run, instinctively acting on her need to get away, to escape from all the staring eyes that knew all that was most private to her.

She saw people stand up, turning towards her as she blundered down the aisle. Panic drove her legs faster. She burst through the doors, startling a group of photographers who followed her like hounds, barking at her, clicking their cameras. Footsteps...voices shouting behind her...her heart thumping with fear, with hate, with love that could never be...and at last in front of her were the steps to the street, the steps that would take her away from the vultures that wanted to peck at her, peck at all that had been so horribly exposed.

Someone caught her. 'Let me go! Let me go!' she sobbed, struggling desperately to free herself.

'Jessica!'

It was Gideon. Gideon's hands turning her around, Gideon's arms enclosing her, crushing her to him.

CHAPTER THIRTEEN

THE frantic compulsion that had driven Jessica from the courtroom melted into an overwhelming weakness. Her legs turned to jelly and she sagged against Gideon, wanting nothing else but to be held in the strong haven of his embrace. But shame forced a protest. 'No...no...' she sobbed in bitter despair.

'I'll never let you go, Jessica, do you hear? Never!' he declared with passionate vehemence. 'You said you loved me.'

'Oh, Gideon,' Jessica dragged out painfully. 'You don't have to...'

'Jessica, look at me!'

One arm tightened around her like a vice as he lifted his other hand to her chin and forced her head up. His eyes blazed into hers with an intensity of feeling that stilled the sickening turmoil inside her.

'I love you. Do you understand? I love you, and nothing means more to me than you do, Jessica. I hope to God you can forgive me for putting you through that appalling ordeal. If only I'd known what I was asking of you, I would never have asked it. Never! I would have given them Pillatoro rather than have you go through that.'

Magic words. Healing, beautiful words. And she could not doubt that Gideon meant them. The torment in his eyes was for her. He loved her, loved her as deeply as she loved him. And nothing else mattered.

'Oh, Gideon,' she breathed, and it was a breath of love that did not even recognise there was anything to forgive. He was with her. He wanted to be with her more than anything else in the world. She let her head drop on to his shoulder and gave herself into his keeping.

'And I want you as my wife, Jessica,' he said even more passionately. 'How could you think I would...'

A sardonic laugh broke through the swirl of emotion that bound them together. 'You're more a fool than I thought you, Cavilha,' Rex Anderson's voice sneered.

Gideon stiffened, his whole body vibrating with the tension of a wild animal about to spring. His dark face was suffused with a barbaric rage that should have frightened Rex. It frightened Jessica. But her erstwhile lover couldn't resist spitting some more bile.

'I'll discredit that bitch and her convenient discovery in front of...'

Even as Gideon was disengaging himself from Jessica, a bull-like roar drowned out Rex's last words. The people behind him were suddenly swept aside. Two great hands wrapped around Rex's neck and he was lifted off his feet and shaken. 'You should have been throttled at birth, you bastard!' Sam growled, terrible in his fury, his face contorted with absolute rage. 'And I intend to do it now.'

Unintelligible noises gurgled from Rex Anderson's throat. His arms flailed at the big man, but made no impact. Other people tried to pull Sam away, but he shrugged them off like flies.

Jessica looked up at Gideon and fear clutched at her heart. There was no thought of rescue for Rex Anderson on his face. His jaw was clenched with the same fierce need for violence which was driving Sam, and should Sam let go, Gideon was all stoked up to take over.

It was Bernadette who struck a note of sanity. She pushed her way to Sam and plucked urgently at his arm. 'Stop it, Sam! You'll kill him!' she screamed.

Her frantic cry caught his attention. 'You're right, Bernadette. A quick death is too good for him. He should die slowly.'

Sam set Rex down on his feet, removed one hand from his throat, drew back his arm and smashed a mighty clenched fist into Rex's jaw. He went flying backwards. People scattered out of the way.

'Get up, you scum!' Sam bellowed at him. 'Get up and fight! I'm not finished with you yet.'

Rex stayed down. 'This'll cost you, Cavilha,' he croaked, gingerly feeling his throat and jaw.

'Not as much as it'll cost you!' Sam spat, bouncing away the few hardy men who tried to stop him from a further assault.

Rex took one look at the murderous rage on Sam's face, scrambled to his feet and turned tail, half stumbling down the steps in his haste to escape.

'That's right! Scuttle away to the hole you crawled out of!' Sam yelled down at him in monumental disgust.

Bernadette flung her arms around his waist. 'Let him go, Sam. Please. It won't do any good.'

'Ah, but it did me a lot of good, Bernadette,' he grated, and hugged the girl in rough comfort.

Then he turned to where Gideon and Jessica were still standing and slowly walked over to them. He did not look at Jessica. His gaze locked on to Gideon's, questioning, demanding. 'In my whole life I've never asked you for anything, Gideon. Never. But I'm asking now. Will you look after Jessica?'

Gideon stiffened. Jessica sensed the pain which coursed through him, the pain of understanding what Sam was feeling, but neither his face nor Sam's revealed any emotion now. People were watching in avid curiosity, lapping up the drama of the moment. Gideon looked back at his brother with steady intensity. 'All my life, Sam,' he replied solemnly.

Sam nodded, sucked in a deep breath and clasped his brother's shoulder. 'I'm glad for you. I truly am. Take care of her, Gideon. I'll finish this up with Pembroke and go on home to Pillatoro.'

'Thank you, Sam,' Gideon murmured huskily, his voice breaking for a moment, revealing how deeply he was moved by Sam's generosity.

'It'll be all right, Gideon. I'll look after everything. For you...and Jessica. Come back when you're ready.' He turned and smiled down at Bernadette who stood by, a hopelessly forlorn look on her lovely face. 'Come on, tiger,' he said with warm indulgence. 'You can protect me from breaking a few more heads.'

A lovely smile of hope was lifted to him and Bernadette threw her arms around the big man's waist. 'I'll come back to Pillatoro with you, Sam. Keep you company.'

'Sure. Why not? Might get in a bit of sailing,' he said, and with his arm curved affectionately around Bernadette's shoulders, they walked off together.

Jessica was conscious of television cameras rolling. They had wanted publicity for Pillatoro, but not this sensational type of muck-raking. Everything that had happened today would be splashed across the newspapers tomorrow. With a heavy sigh she looked up at the man she loved, and love looked back at her, and it didn't matter what was printed.

'Gideon...' It was Hal Chissolm. 'Car's waiting for you at the bottom of the steps, ready to go.'

'Thanks, Hal.'

And while attention was still following Sam, Gideon and Hal hurried Jessica down the steps to the limousine. She was bundled into the back seat. Gideon stepped in after her. Hal slammed the door. 'Good luck,' he called softly as the driver accelerated away from the crowd which was spilling down the steps after them.

'Where are we going?' Jessica asked breathlessly.

'Where you'll be safe and we can be alone,' Gideon replied, then kissed her with a passion which answered every other question.

Jessica felt positively light-headed. That Gideon should declare his love for her so publicly and with such unwavering conviction after she had been stripped naked in front of everyone...it was the kind of love she had dreamed of.

He hugged her to him with a fierce protectiveness as he feathered kisses over her face, speaking in tortured little bursts. 'I won't let anyone near you, Jessica. Once we're in the hotel we'll shut the world out. No calls. No people. Just you and me. Let the jackals howl. They won't touch us.'

'Oh, Gideon,' she whispered with all the love in her heart. 'I don't mind any more. It was worth any price to be with you like this.'

'No one will ever do that to you again,' he swore, with such menace in his voice that Jessica shivered.

The car slowed to a halt. The chauffeur jumped out to hold the door open for them and at the same instant, staff streamed out from the hotel, virtually forming a guard for them. Reporters who had followed the car were muscled out of the way as Gideon raced Jessica into the foyer. The hotel doors were closed behind them and the hotel manager met them and ushered them into a waiting lift.

'Mr Chissolm warned us,' he informed them as they rode up to Gideon's suite. 'We'll ensure your privacy, Mr Cavilha.'

'Thank you. Hold all calls until I tell you otherwise,' Gideon ordered peremptorily.

'Anything else, sir?'

'A man patrolling the floor outside my suite. Any staff entering the suite to have their identity checked beforehand.'

'Certainly, Mr Cavilha. I'll see to that immediately.'

The lift came to a halt, the doors rolled open, and the hotel manager saw them safely to their suite before departing to effect Gideon's requirements.

With the door securely locked behind them, Gideon suddenly scooped Jessica up in his arms and carried her through to the bedroom. There on

the bed he had given to her when Rex had shut her
out of his life, Gideon gently laid her down.

'I'll get you a glass of cognac.'

'No.' Jessica clutched his arm as he would have
moved away from her. His eyes stabbed back at her
in quick concern. 'I don't want anything, Gideon,'
she said softly. 'Only you.'

He sank down on the bed beside her and very
slowly, with loving care, he removed her hairpins
and loosened the long coils of hair, running his
fingers through the silky tresses with a tenderness
that was more poignant than any speech. His gaze
drifted slowly over her face as if wanting to redis-
cover and memorise every line and plane, and never
had Jessica seen his eyes so soft. When he finally
spoke, his voice vibrated with his feeling for her.

'I want you as I've never wanted any other
woman, Jessica. God knows I loved Alison as much
as any man possibly could, but what I feel for
you...' He drew back a little, caressing her with
eyes that were strangely vulnerable. 'I belong to
you. You belong to me. That's how it is, isn't it?'

'Yes,' she whispered.

His eyes searched hers, needing the love that
glowed there for him. 'I want you to know it all,
Jessica. Alison would never have been capable of
doing what you've done for me. That night on the
parapet...she wouldn't have come to me as you
did. She wouldn't have shared with me what you've
shared with me. She couldn't have stood up for me
in a courtroom and endured what you endured.'

He shook his head in pained memory. 'She did
not have your strength, Jessica. I loved her for what
she was; but although we were married and she bore

my children, I remained apart from her. She was beside me, but not with me. She needed me, but she never really saw or recognised my needs. But you, Jessica, you answer all of them. And I love you more deeply than any words can express.'

She wound her arms around his neck and pulled him down on to the bed with her. 'Then make love with me, Gideon. I want you to,' she breathed happily.

He smiled at her with all the love that had been bottled up in his heart, and as his mouth gently brushed across hers, he said her name as no one else could ever say it, 'Jessica...Jessica...Jessica...'

'I love you, Gideon,' she answered simply.

He kissed her then, kissed her with a vehemence that transmitted all the need in his soul that had waited so long to find its fulfilment. And Jessica gave herself, wanting what he wanted, committing herself totally to the union which was a joyous celebration of their belonging, one to the other, together, for as long as they should live.

When the demands of love and need had been fully met and satisfied, they lay in each other's arms, supremely content to express themselves more quietly. Jessica lightly caressed the face which was so inexpressibly dear to her. It was no longer closed to her, no longer inscrutable. She knew the man behind it intimately. She placed gentle fingers on his lips.

'We'll have children, Gideon.'

'Yes,' he murmured happily, kissing her fingers.

'And Pillatoro will go on.'

'Yes,' he said with even more satisfaction. 'It's been waiting for you, Jessica, and now it has a heart again.' He wound his fingers through her long hair and tugged her down to him. 'My love, my wife, my life,' he murmured, kissing the words into the heart that beat all the more strongly because he held it.

POSTSCRIPT

ON Monday, 6th December, 1986, at 3 p.m., Justice Legge handed down a judgement in the Supreme Court restraining the Minister for the Environment from resuming Pillatoro, together with an order that the Cavilha family be left in peace. The Government did not appeal against this judgement.

Harlequin Presents

Coming Next Month

1111 AN AWAKENING DESIRE Helen Bianchin
Emma, recently widowed, isn't looking for romance. But a visit to her late husband Marc's grandparents in Italy seems like a good first step in picking up the pieces of her life. She certainly isn't ready to deal with a man like Nick Castelli!

1112 STRAY LADY Vanessa Grant
Since her husband's death, George has felt that she doesn't belong anywhere anymore. Then Lyle rescues her from her smashed sailboat and makes her feel at home in the lighthouse. But to kindhearted Lyle is she just another stray?

1113 LEVELLING THE SCORE Penny Jordan
Jenna had once loved Simon Townsend—a mere teenage crush, but he has never let her forget it. So when she has a chance for revenge, she takes it. Simon, however, has his own methods of retaliation....

1114 THE WILDER SHORES OF LOVE Madeleine Ker
She'd never thought it would happen to her—but almost without knowing it Margot Prescott turns from a detached reporter of the drug scene to an addict. Adam Korda saves her. But the freer she becomes of the drug, the more attached she becomes to Adam.

1115 STORM CLOUD MARRIAGE Roberta Leigh
Sandra has always known Randall Pearson. He was her father's faceless deputy, and has only once surprised her. One night he asked her to marry him. She'd refused then, of course, but now four years later Sandra is doing the proposing!

1116 MIRACLE MAN Joanna Mansell
Lacey is happy with her safe, sexless relationship with her boss—Marcus Caradin of Caradin Tours. Then he asks her to go on a business trip with him. Suddenly, in the exotic surroundings of India and Nepal, it isn't safe anymore....

1117 ONE CHANCE AT LOVE Carole Mortimer
Dizzy's family background made her wary of commitment. Zach Bennett is the first man to make her want to throw caution to the winds. But her position is awkward. Because of a promise, she has to conceal her real nature from Zach.

1118 THERE IS NO TOMORROW Yvonne Whittal
Despite her plea of innocence, Revil Bradstone despises Alexa because he'd once caught her in a compromising situation. Now he threatens vengeance through her employer. Desperate, Alexa is ready to promise him anything!

Available in October wherever paperback books are sold, or through Harlequin Reader Service:

In the U.S.
901 Fuhrmann Blvd.
P.O. Box 1397
Buffalo, N.Y. 14240-1397

In Canada
P.O. Box 603
Fort Erie, Ontario
L2A 5X3

ATTRACTIVE, SPACE SAVING BOOK RACK

Display your most prized novels on this handsome and sturdy book rack. The hand-rubbed walnut finish will blend into your library decor with quiet elegance, providing a practical organizer for your favorite hard-or soft-covered books.

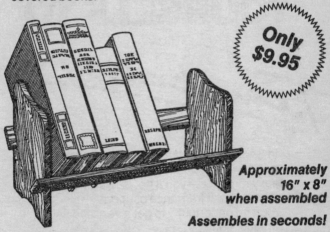

Only $9.95

Approximately 16" x 8" when assembled

Assembles in seconds!

To order, rush your name, address and zip code, along with a check or money order for $10.70* ($9.95 plus 75¢ postage and handling) payable to *Harlequin Reader Service*:

Harlequin Reader Service
Book Rack Offer
901 Fuhrmann Blvd.
P.O. Box 1396
Buffalo, NY 14269-1396

Offer not available in Canada.

BKR-1A

*New York and Iowa residents add appropriate sales tax.